"Fitzwater provides an entertaining (and for aspiring writers, frustratingly familiar) look at the world of writing and publishing."

—*Publishers Weekly*

"Expertly plotted . . . Ingenious and satisfying."
—*The Mystery Review*

By Judy Fitzwater
Published by Ballantine Books:

DYING TO GET PUBLISHED
DYING TO GET EVEN
DYING FOR A CLUE

Books published by The Ballantine Publishing Group
are available at quantity discounts on bulk purchases
for premium, educational, fund-raising, and special
sales use. For details, please call 1-800-733-3000.

DYING TO REMEMBER

Judy Fitzwater

FAWCETT BOOKS • NEW YORK

A Fawcett Book
Published by The Ballantine Publishing Group
Copyright © 2000 by Judy Fitzwater

www.randomhouse.com/BB/

Library of Congress Catalog Card Number: 00-103808

ISBN 0-449-00639-5

Manufactured in the United States of America

First Edition: August 2000

10 9 8 7 6 5 4 3 2 1

For Anastasia and Miellyn
May all your reunions be happy

I am fortunate to have wonderful people surround me as I write:

Larry, Miellyn, and Anastasia, who lend their support and total confidence that I will always find a way to pull together whatever story I am currently working on.

My editor Joe Blades, whose enthusiasm is a rare and truly appreciated gift.

Patricia Peters, who is a joy to work with.

My sisters in writing: Robyn Amos, Ann Kline, Vicki Singer, and Karen Smith, whose talent shines through my work as well as theirs.

Patricia Gagne, Ryan Kelly, and Melynda McBeth, who were generous with their helpful suggestions.

Please note my apologies to all the heroic men named Wilbur.

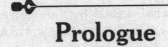

Prologue

Twelve Years Ago

"Geez, Danny, how many hands do you have?" Jennifer Marsh swatted at her date's ear and managed to push herself back against the passenger door of the old Chevrolet, seriously wrinkling the ice-blue satin of her prom gown. The guy was an octopus. When they'd left to get away from the scene his former girlfriend was making in the gym, she'd had something more subtle in mind, like a few stolen kisses, not an all-out grab fest or a game of tonsil hockey.

"Aw, c'mon, Jen. You know how I feel about you."

She stared at those gorgeous dark brown eyes and that dark wavy hair, and her heart skipped a beat. The streetlight near the school parking lot cast an eerie silver glow across the unshadowed part of his face. He did care. She could tell. But about what?

Without warning, Danny dove for her neck, and she ducked to her right, up against the glove compartment. He bumped his head on the door and cursed.

"Keep it up and you're going to tear your tuxedo. It *is* rented, isn't it?"

"Okay, okay. Maybe I'm taking this a little too fast." Danny sat back behind the wheel and rubbed the bruise on his forehead. "What say we talk a little?"

1

Jennifer righted herself in the seat and stared out the windshield at the school's loading dock, wondering why her image of this night, the night of her senior prom, bore such little resemblance to reality.

At least her hair had survived. But then, the mass of taffy brown curls across the back of her head was so full of hair spray it would take a major explosion to move it.

Fingering the crumpled petals on the rosebud cluster of her corsage, she remembered how beautiful it had looked when he'd pinned it to her gown at her house. Red roses. The symbol of true love.

She felt Danny's hand find hers, lacing his fingers with her own. They sat there quietly, neither daring to say a word or even steal a glance. A sweet sadness tugged at her heart. Maybe, somehow, the evening might still be saved. Any second, Danny might turn to her and say exactly the right words. . . .

The blow to the driver's side window made her jump and shot a spear of terror through Jennifer's heart, filling her mind with every scene from every horror movie she'd ever seen about young lovers alone in a car late at night.

She forced herself to look. A stocky young man stared through the glass, his shaggy brown hair falling in his face. He hit the window with his fist a second time, the white sleeve of his letter man's jacket flat against the glass. At least he didn't have a hook.

"Hey, Buckner. Need your help, man."

Danny opened the door a crack, allowing a wisp of cool night air to rush in.

"It's my dad's car, man. Break that window and I'll break your head," Danny told him. Then he nodded in her direction. "Can't you see I'm busy? Catch me later."

As the boy turned toward the light, Jennifer recognized him

as one of the guys Danny hung out with, one she didn't particularly care for. He had what looked like panic on his face.

"Not later. Now, Danny boy," he insisted, wedging his shoulder between the open door and the car's frame. "You gotta come. I ain't goin' away. You gotta help, man."

"You guys need to lighten up. It's the senior prom, for God's sake." Danny muttered several nasty oaths and then gave her hand a quick squeeze. "Lock the doors. I'll be right back. I promise."

And then he was gone, leaving her to stare into the creepy darkness, waiting. Shivering. Alone. Waiting, all by herself, past the far end of the school parking lot on a spring Georgia night, the night that was supposed to be the highlight of her young life.

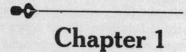

Chapter 1

High school. The words made Jennifer Marsh shudder. She'd left all thoughts of it behind her twelve years ago, and she wasn't about to go back. Not for love, not for money, and certainly not for a plate of fettuccine Alfredo and a chocolate sundae.

"It's *your* ten-year reunion," Jennifer reminded Leigh Ann as calmly as she could, across the small, round table at Luigi's, irritated that she'd been suckered into a lunch date with a secret agenda. She'd actually put on a skirt and panty hose for this?

She should have known something was up when Leigh Ann had offered to treat. "You don't need me to go with you, and I certainly have no desire to see any of those people ever again."

"I think you just insulted me. *I'm* one of those people," Leigh Ann reminded her, tugging at the lapel of her jade-colored suit. The petite brunette scooped up a spoonful of syrup, drizzled it over her vanilla ice cream, and kept her green eyes focused on the thin stream of chocolate. Luigi kept the syrup just for her. Sundaes weren't on the menu.

"It's for all classes," Leigh Ann went on, "like it always is, so they can get a big enough crowd to warrant using the school gym. Everybody's going to be there."

Leigh Ann cleared her throat. "Danny Buckner is coming. He does every year, just waiting for you to show up. I'm sure he's dying to see you again."

The mention of Danny's name, even all these years later, sent a twinge through her heart.

She grabbed Leigh Ann's spoon away from her, dripping fudge on the white tablecloth, and shook it at her. "Why you would think I'd still be interested in the likes of Danny Buckner—"

A lady at the next table raised an eyebrow, and Jennifer abruptly stopped talking.

Leigh Ann rolled her eyes. "You were smitten with the boy, Jen."

"Smitten? What kind of word is that?" Jennifer demanded in a loud whisper. "People haven't been 'smitten' for the last fifty years. Besides, he's married."

"Well yeah, to Sheena Cassidy. But I always considered that a temporary condition."

If looks could burn, Leigh Ann would have gone up in flames. "Ten years can hardly be considered temporary," Jennifer pointed out.

Leigh Ann held up her hands in defense. "You are *so* touchy. Besides, I was just stating my opinion. I certainly wasn't suggesting that you start something up with him again. I just thought you might be curious, after all these years, to know how he turned out."

Jennifer dropped her gaze. She could almost feel her friend studying her face, which must be glowing a soft pink if the heat she felt in her cheeks was any indication.

"Sheena kind of did a number on you, didn't she?" Leigh Ann observed.

That was an understatement. Once Sheena realized Danny had set his sights on Jennifer, her only mission was to turn Jennifer's life into a living hell. No boy could possibly be worth going through all that. And Jennifer's inability to handle the situation was one of the true regrets of her life.

"But you still went to the senior prom with him," Leigh Ann reminded her.

Jennifer dropped the spoon back into Leigh Ann's stemmed ice cream glass and turned an even brighter red. She couldn't tell Leigh Ann it was as much an act of revenge as a fulfillment of a crush. Evil, terrible revenge against Sheena for all the horrible things that short-skirted, mean-to-the-bone junior squad cheerleader had done to her. And she'd paid for that revenge dearly.

Prom night had been one of the worst nights of her life. And not just because Sheena had tried to take Danny away from her on the dance floor, or because she'd come home to a house with toilet paper streaming from the trees.

"I think you should go," Leigh Ann insisted with bright eyes, scooping up another bite of sundae. "You've got your college degree, you're writing your books, you're working with Dee Dee in her catering business making those vegetable flower wreaths that are true works of art, you've got no gray in your hair and no lines in your face except when you smile really big, you haven't gained an ounce, and you've got all your teeth."

"All my teeth? I'm only thir—" The word stuck in her throat. She'd found no graceful way to ease into the next decade of her life. It'd come upon her like a tiger in the night, ripping her youth from her and leaving her in shock. Like it or not, she was one of the grown-ups now.

And her life plan—to have her mystery writing career well under way by this time—was all askew. If she gave in and went to the reunion, what would she say when people asked her what she did for a living? She could hardly tell them she was a wannabe—with nine unpublished manuscripts gathering dust in her closet and more rejection slips than *Gone with the Wind* had pages.

"What do you plan to tell them about *your* writing?" Jennifer asked.

A twinkle sparked in Leigh Ann's eye as she savored the ice cream on her tongue. "Writing? Who's going to be talking about writing?"

She knew better than to go anywhere with Leigh Ann, even if Leigh Ann was one of her dearest friends and a member of her writers' group. Leigh Ann was always on the prowl. She lived and breathed the romance she wrote, and yet . . .

Jennifer studied Leigh Ann's tiny, doll-like features. What was it that made love so elusive for her? Why did she keep it on such a superficial, primitive attraction level? Why did she have such commitment issues?

And why was she so hot to go to this reunion? They'd known each other in high school, but not well. Had there been someone, maybe back then, when most insecurities are formed . . .

"Besides, I'm thinking about writing a book about old flames," Leigh Ann said. "You know, high school sweethearts who find each other years later. Something a lot of people can relate to."

Two years ago Jennifer had started writing a book of her own based on her high school experiences, but it was no love story. It had turned into something more along the lines of *Scream* or *Prom Night*. She'd put it away. Obviously, she had issues, and Leigh Ann should realize that some unresolved problems were better left that way, before they had a chance to rise up and bite her again.

"All I'm asking is that you think about it," Leigh Ann said.

"It doesn't matter anyway. I'm sure it's too late to register."

"Not to worry. I already sent in your fee along with mine."

"You what?" Jennifer demanded.

But Leigh Ann totally ignored her. Glancing at her watch, she let out a small squeal and pulled her purse from under her chair. "You could even bring Sam with you if you want. You're allowed one guest, and who wouldn't want to be seen with a good-looking investigative reporter from *The Macon Telegraph*? Say, if you can't go, you think Sam might—"

Jennifer shot her another dangerous look.

"I was just kidding." Leigh Ann grabbed her glass and gulped one final glug of water. "Gotta go. My boss will be tapping her foot waiting for me. Unlike *some* people, I have a day job. Remember, Saturday night, seven o'clock. I'll pick you up a little before."

Jennifer opened her mouth to protest, but Leigh Ann was already out the door, leaving Jennifer staring after her.

Leigh Ann could go if she wanted to, but Jennifer had no intentions of ever again setting foot across the threshold of Riverside High School.

Chapter 2

Jennifer stared at the note that had come in the morning's mail, her hand trembling. Seeing Danny Buckner's scrawled handwriting still made her heart skip a beat. Despite how she'd tried to minimize their relationship to Leigh Ann, she'd had a huge crush on Danny. They'd had nothing in common except a major teenage chemical attraction, but in many ways he was her first, however brief, love.

And now he was asking for her help.

Yo, Jen. Read in the newspaper about you working for that private detective, Johnny Zeeman. Really cool. Glad to see you're still in town. Thought you might be coming to the reunion Saturday night and maybe you could spare me a few minutes. Something's come back up, something I thought was long over and done. Guess not. Hope to see you Saturday. Love you. Danny.

What could have "come back up," and why would Danny be contacting her, of all people? Did he think she had some kind of private eye expertise? If he did, he was going to be sorely disappointed. Her adventure with Johnny Zeeman had been a one-shot, involuntary involvement in a case that had tangled around her like a spiderweb.

Jennifer sank onto the couch in her small apartment and stared into space. Muffy, her greyhound, snuggled about her feet, playing with her shoelaces, but she hardly noticed. She and Danny had officially dated, if she remembered correctly (and she did), for no more than a couple of weeks, although he'd been seriously interested for closer to six months. Once Sheena had figured out Danny was about to stray, she'd started a campaign to smear Jennifer and make her life miserable.

But all that was beside the point. What could have happened involving Danny that would be coming back up *now*?

Something even worse than being stranded at school in that old Chevrolet on prom night? She'd waited close to forty minutes before finally deciding Danny wasn't coming back. Humiliated, she'd gone inside the building and called her father to come get her. Even now, just thinking about it made her shudder. At least her dad had the sensitivity not to ask what happened. He'd simply picked her up and driven her home. He hadn't even said a word about the toilet paper in the trees.

Danny the Worm had found her Monday morning, trapping her between the end locker and the science room door. He groveled and pleaded, even got down on his knee at one point, which gave her the opportunity to step over him and get the heck out of there. She'd never been able to forgive him. The hurt was too deep.

Through all his expressions of remorse, Danny never told her what he'd done that night. Maybe if he had, things would have been different. And maybe not. She wasn't sure she wanted to know. Not then and not now. Especially if he'd somehow wound up spending the rest of that night with Sheena.

But maybe what Danny wanted to talk to her about had nothing to do with that night. She could at least hope.

She stuffed the paper back into its envelope, sighed, absently untangled Muffy's incisors from her shoelaces, and rubbed the dog behind the ears.

She needed to get going, but she was having trouble even getting off the couch. She was late and Dee Dee would be calling any minute wondering what had happened to her. She had two large vegetable rings to arrange, tomatoes to stuff, and a shrimp tree to put together for a birthday party in Wimbish Woods, not to mention the broccoli-raisin-peanut salad that had to be prepared at the last minute to keep its flavor. It all had to be in Dee Dee's van no later than five o'clock.

She didn't have time to think about Danny Buckner, she reasoned. Besides, she owed him absolutely nothing. She was involved with Sam now. Sam, who was smart, funny, endearing, honest, infuriating, and, in so many ways, really good for her. But Danny was special. She could count on three fingers the number of guys who had ever taken her breath away, and Danny had been the first.

The reunion was only one night of her life. What could it hurt to talk to him?

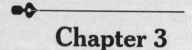

Chapter 3

Going back to high school was like having Thanksgiving with family. Jennifer was painfully aware that if she wasn't careful, she could lose all the progress she'd made in the past twelve years, progress she was holding onto as tightly as Leigh Ann would let her.

The phone rang again. "What do you think?" Leigh Ann's voice gasped. "Should I wear the forest-green knit, the black chiffon, or the red satin?"

"It's a reunion, Leigh, not the prom. Go with the knit."

"But—"

Jennifer growled, trying to negotiate a pair of honey-beige panty hose over one knee while balancing on one foot. Hugging the phone between her ear and her shoulder, she tried to keep Muffy, who seemed convinced she was Jennifer's dresser, away from the delicate nylon mesh. "Why did you call me if you didn't want my opinion?"

"I do, only—"

"Just wear whatever you want. Look, I've got to get dressed, too. See you later."

"Okay, but—"

"Later." She hung up the phone, hoping she wasn't too rude, but this was already Leigh Ann's fourth call in the last twenty minutes. The first was to ask whether she should wear her hair up or down, the second to ask if blue or gold fingernail polish was too hip for people their age, and the third had to do with liquid versus pencil eyeliner. As if she would know the difference.

She made a final tug of the panty hose over her hips and rued the fact that Leigh Ann—and Danny's letter—had snookered her into going in the first place. Now, after that phone call, she had to wonder if her own royal-blue jersey was appropriate. Two minutes ago she'd been convinced it was the perfect choice.

She wiggled into her slip, Muffy catching the hem in her teeth and pulling the silky fabric hard into place, just as the phone rang again.

"What is it this time?" Jennifer demanded, grabbing up the receiver and stretching as far as the cord would allow so she could shove Muffy out the bedroom door and close it behind her.

"Did you read the newspaper today?"

"Cut to the chase, Leigh Ann."

"Your horoscope."

"How old are you?"

"Listen to this: 'Take that invitation. Old acquaintances come back into your life in ways you never imagined possible.' See? You were meant to go."

"I'm going, remember? You don't have to sell me on it anymore. But if you don't stop calling me, I'm going to miss the whole reunion because you won't let me get ready. Understand?"

"Want to hear mine?"

"No."

"Okay, then. Be like that. See you at 6:45."

Jennifer dropped the receiver back into its cradle and wondered exactly why Leigh Ann was so nervous about the reunion, and why she was allowing that nervousness to creep across the phone lines. All her talk of dresses, hair, and horoscopes stirred up more memories of another night so many years ago that had started out a little too perfect to be true.

She shook her head. She didn't have time to think about anything now. She was running way too late, and too much thought threatened her promise to go. She grabbed her dress off the bed and had no more gotten herself tangled in the blue jersey, searching for an armhole, when the phone rang yet again. She snatched up the receiver with the one hand that had successfully found its way through the sleeve.

"This is getting really old, Leigh Ann," she sputtered.

"You all right?" It was Sam.

"Hold on for two seconds." She let the phone drop onto the bed, slipped her other arm into the sleeve, and pulled the zipper up in back. She was dressed, at least technically.

"Okay, I'm back."

"I thought I'd make that offer one more time. Want me to come to the reunion with you?"

It was tempting, but the dangers were too great. If she began to slip back into her awkward, emotionally vulnerable, nerdish, teenage state, she certainly didn't need witnesses, especially not one she cared about as much as Sam.

"No. I'll be fine. But tell you what, I don't expect to stay too long. Could we get together later, maybe for some coffee?"

"Sounds good to me."

She said goodbye, hung up the phone, sat down on the side of the bed and tapped her index finger against her bottom lip. Thoughts she had tried to avoid for years were crowding her mind, thoughts that were even more unsettling than her memories of Danny and Sheena. She didn't want to go to the reunion because she didn't want to be reminded of Jimmy Mitchell.

He had been younger than her—a sixteen-year-old

sophomore—fairly quiet and pretty nondescript, with a way of popping up when he was least expected. She would never have given him a second thought, not then, not now, if, on the night of her senior prom, he hadn't disappeared off the face of the earth.

Chapter 4

"Nice," Leigh Ann commented, nodding at the navy-blue-and-silver balloons tied to paper-covered tables, folding chairs, and every available post in the gym. More balloons formed an arch atop a portable stage that had been added to one end of the room. Above the arch, dark blue netting sporting large silver stars cascaded from the rafters. The words A NIGHT TO REMEMBER hung as though suspended in space above it all.

"Wasn't that the title of that old movie about the *Titanic*?" Jennifer asked.

"No, silly. That was the theme for my senior prom, ten years ago. I'd forgotten. It's kind of neat, don't you think?"

"I thought this reunion was for all classes."

"It is. But my class is special."

"What about the people celebrating their twentieth and thirtieth reunions?"

"They're special, too, but they weren't on the planning committee. By the way," Leigh Ann added, "I'm glad you went with the blue, even if it does kind of get lost with the decorations." She nodded toward Jennifer's dress, immediately making Jennifer wish she'd opted for blue jeans and a sweatshirt.

The gym was already full of people, people Jennifer could

16

swear she'd never seen before. Could Leigh Ann have gotten the date wrong? Probably not, what with her prom recreated right before their eyes. But all these people looked, well, *old*.

A big WELCOME sign hung from the bleachers at the other end of the room over a long refreshment table sporting a huge decorated cake welcoming the special guests, the tenth-year class. A faded strawberry blonde with an orchid corsage pinned to the lapel of her lavender suit was ladling out punch along with cake and big dimpled smiles. She looked so stable, so mature, so, ohmygosh . . . She looked like a younger version of Flo Steiner's mother.

The woman caught Jennifer's eye, dropped her ladle, and came straight for her with outstretched arms, leaving the guests lined up for refreshments to fend for themselves. She pulled Jennifer into a bear hug, squishing her orchid.

"I can't believe it! It's Jennifer Marsh!" The woman let loose, then grabbed both Jennifer's hands and bounced up and down, most peculiar in what appeared to be a mature adult. "Where the heck have you been? I don't think I've seen you since—"

"The day we graduated," Jennifer finished, struggling out of the woman's grasp. They'd been in chorus together, which made them friends of a sort, but not close enough to walk across the football field to say hello. Seems time had brought them closer.

"You must have left Macon," Flo chastised. The otherwise-you-would-have-called-me part was left unspoken.

"Just to go to college. I've been back for the past eight years."

"Really? Well, it's hard to believe we haven't run into each other at least once at the Food Lion."

Now that she thought about it, she probably had seen Flo

a few times, mistaking her for her mother. She certainly wasn't avoiding her, not like she was Danny and Sheena, but Macon wasn't big enough not to have at least spied a few of her former classmates over the past years.

"How many kids you got?" Flo asked.

Ah, yes. Children. She could fake success, a career, even a committed relationship, but offspring? She hardly thought it wise to share the fact that although she had none, her first-born-to-be was already named Jaimie and someone with whom she occasionally conversed. Sort of like an imaginary friend, only for grown-ups.

"No kids. No husband," Jennifer confessed.

"You poor thing," Flo gushed.

Jennifer pursed her lips and threw an I'm-not-going-to-forgive-you-for-this glare at Leigh Ann, who was paying no attention whatsoever to the conversation. Instead, she was staring across the gym, her mouth open, her eyes wide.

Jennifer followed her gaze.

Near the foot of the stage, Sheena Cassidy Buckner literally glowed in a spaghetti-strapped, red-silk affair that flattered her trim, abs-of-steel figure. Her long, fair curls, with a wave down one side, lay softly on her shoulders. She was beautiful, every bit as beautiful as she'd been at sixteen. And probably just as evil, Jennifer thought, tasting bile in her throat. She felt a flush color her face as adrenaline swept through her body, putting every nerve on edge. Even after all these years.

Jennifer growled. The woman could at least have had the decency to age poorly. Was there no justice in this world?

Flo's overzealous enthusiasm suddenly seemed far more inviting, and her conversation, whatever it was, far more interesting. Jennifer started to turn back, but her peripheral vision caught sight of a familiar figure standing not too far from Sheena. Jennifer turned to stare.

Danny. Darned if he didn't still have that black curl twisted down the middle of his forehead. He looked heavier than he had back then, but that was to his credit. He'd been a skinny kid. He had a mustache. That was new. And no smile. That was new, too. She wondered if the charm was still there. It had been the one constant in Danny's character.

He was standing with three men, each holding a bottle of beer. She recognized them—some easier than others—as Seth Yarborough, Al Carpenter, and Mick Farmer. Danny's old high school crowd. They'd been close to inseparable back then, and they looked almost as tight right now.

Danny turned and looked straight at her. She could feel the color rise again in her cheeks. Not taking his eyes off her, he handed his beer to one of the guys, then broke from the group, went over to Sheena and leaned down to say something in her ear. Then he headed rapidly toward Jennifer, across the sleek, hardwood gymnasium floor.

Leaving Sheena staring straight at her with a strange look of half anger and half . . . what? Fear?

Jennifer whirled on Leigh Ann, leaving Flo to coo at her back. "Okay. We came, we visited. Time to go now."

"But Danny's coming this—"

She grabbed Leigh Ann's arm and tugged her through the crowd toward the closest doors. She'd thought she could handle this. She *ought* to be able to handle this. What was she? Some kind of cream puff?

Absolutely.

She simply couldn't bring herself to talk to a man who had married Sheena Cassidy. Whatever he might have seen in her—besides the hair, the face, and the figure—it couldn't possibly be enough to overlook that low-down, mean, rotten core.

Jennifer's mother had always told her, "When you see someone mistreating someone else, don't think you're immune. You have that person as a friend, and they'll get around to you eventually."

So had Sheena gotten around to Danny? Ten years was a long time. Yet he had stayed. Which begged the question, why? How well had she ever known Danny Buckner?

"Whoa!" Leigh Ann shrugged her arm free from Jennifer's grasp and straightened her dress. "Get ahold of yourself! Come on now, deep breaths. You can do it." As though she were Bela Karolyi coaching Kerri Strug through that last great vault at the summer Olympics in Atlanta. Kerri had done it and done it perfectly, but at a price.

"You know what, Leigh Ann? That's the good thing about being a grown-up. Some things you don't have to do."

She slipped through the doors, leaving Leigh Ann and high school behind, to find herself alone in the silence of a hallway, staring at the same gray tile floor, institutional cream walls, and metal lockers, now painted a deep forest green, that she had wrestled with for four years.

If she walked straight down the hallway and took a right at the stairwell, she should come to the front of the building. If she were lucky, the doors would be unlocked. She could slip out and go back around to the parking lot where she could wait for Leigh Ann. After all, how long could she be? Three, four hours, maybe?

Or she could call Sam. Wonderful, sensible, good-hearted Sam. It wouldn't be the first time he'd helped her out of a difficult situation.

There used to be a pay phone around the corner, near the entrance to the auditorium. If she were lucky, it'd still be there. Her footsteps echoed in the emptiness as she started down the corridor.

"Jennifer . . ."

She stopped in mid-step, her breath leaving her, and every nerve in her body suddenly alert. It had been a lot of years since she'd heard that voice.

Chapter 5

Jennifer turned. Danny still looked darned good, even close up. Even in his sport coat and tie. She'd only seen him dressed up once before—that dreadful night. He was older now, with deep lines around his eyes and mouth, but still nice. And taller. He'd added another inch or two since they'd both been eighteen. Either that or she'd forgotten.

"I was hoping I'd find you." He covered the distance between them, and she dropped her gaze. She sensed him looking at her, while the maturity and self-assurance she'd spent years developing dissolved as though they had never existed. She searched for something—maybe a trapdoor—on the gray tile at her feet.

Her heart rumbled in her chest as he caught her index finger with his fist. Slowly, reluctantly, she looked up into his eyes and . . .

And nothing. She felt nothing, except a sweet echo of innocent affection. Her breathing calmed, her heart fell into its regular rhythm, and her adrenaline ebbed. Whatever hold Danny Buckner had had over her for the past twelve years vanished as suddenly as it had descended upon her young self.

She pulled her hand away. "So, Danny, how are you?"

He squinted at her, raising one eyebrow in the process. "Did you get my note?"

"Sure enough. But you seem to have the wrong impression about me. I don't know anything about being a private detective. I only write about that stuff."

"What do you mean you write about it?"

"Well, yeah. As in mystery novels."

"No kidding." He looked impressed and a little less sure of himself. "So what name do you write under?"

Darn. She'd known this would happen. As soon as she told someone she wrote, that person would assume she was published. She couldn't very well tell Danny she had finished so many novels with no hint of publication on the horizon.

"I'm not that far along in the process." The truth, at least.

"Oh." His smile returned, and she could feel some of his confidence return with it.

"What was it you were so anxious to tell me?"

"You do know a private detective." It was as much a question as a statement.

She nodded. Johnny Zeeman was a boozer with an eye for women and a soft heart he kept well hidden. But he did have a shingle and a license that made him, despite his flaws, a bona fide private investigator. And not a bad one at that.

"Are you still working with him?"

"Not exactly, but I do see him occasionally. He had me out on the firing range a few weeks ago. He insisted I get a gun and a permit. Can you imagine me armed?"

"It's a scary thought," he confessed.

"Do you need a P.I.?"

He offered a wry smile and pushed the curl off his forehead, but it immediately bounced back. Some things refuse to change.

"Maybe. Do you remember the night of—"

"Hey, hey, hey! Danny boy! So this is where you've been hiding."

Danny turned, and Al Carpenter, a big, burly guy in a tan jacket, crushed Danny's fingers in a fierce grip, slapped his shoulder hard with his other hand, and pulled him into one of those quasi-hug, buddy greetings that guys do. Strange, since she'd seen them standing together just minutes before.

Al gave Jennifer a none-too-friendly once-over.

The two men broke apart, but the newcomer continued to hold onto Danny's hand in a possessive shake. "Thought you'd run out on us there for a minute."

Danny shook his head, his face flushed. "Never happen. I was just talking to Jennifer here. You remember Jennifer?"

Jennifer studied Al's face, wondering why she was experiencing such a strong feeling of déjà vu, when, suddenly, it all flooded back. The face, the pounding on the car window, the untimely interruption. It was him. Danny's buddy. The guy who had come after him on prom night.

"Can't say that I do," Al said, letting go of Danny and offering his hand to Jennifer.

Reluctantly, she took it. "And you are . . ." If he wouldn't acknowledge her, she'd be darned if she would acknowledge him. He'd been a big jock with a big mouth who didn't concede any girl's existence who wasn't on the cheerleading or pom squad.

"Al Carpenter, attorney at law." He dug in his coat pocket and handed her a card with his picture on it along with the address and phone number of his office. "You ever get yourself into a legal situation, you give me a call."

"I'll keep it in mind," she told him.

"Good. I've got to steal Danny boy here away for a little while. I'm sure you don't mind."

Mind? She was irritated as heck, not that this guy was

taking Danny away, but that this whole situation had such an annoyingly familiar feel to it.

Danny shot her a solemn look. "I'll find you later. I promise."

She knew all about Danny's promises.

"You going to be around for a while?" he added.

"Not too long. Got a late date," she told him.

Danny opened his mouth, but Al had his shoulders in a stranglehold and was already leading him away.

Jennifer slipped back through the door and into the reunion. She had to find Leigh Ann. Danny Buckner didn't need her, whether he knew it or not, and she didn't intend to give him, or his friends, one more minute of her time.

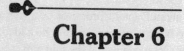

Chapter 6

Leigh Ann, sipping ginger ale and still searching the crowd, was surrounded by a gaggle of quasi-familiar, giggly women. A semicircle of men was keeping a discreet distance, observing the group while nursing their drinks and making small talk. The husbands. The ones who hadn't attended Riverside High School.

Jennifer went straight for Leigh Ann, grabbing her by the arm and pulling her away from the group. "Let's go."

Leigh Ann struggled back, out of her grasp. "Are you at it again? What's with you tonight, Jennifer? You seem fixated on dragging me around by the elbow."

"I don't want to be here," Jennifer assured her in measured, no-nonsense tones.

"Why are you so upset? What the heck did Danny say to you? I saw him follow you into the hall. You want I should set him straight?"

Leigh Ann glanced over toward the foot of the stage, and Jennifer looked, too. Sheena was playing her part well, entertaining former cheerleaders and star jocks, slinging her glass about, laughing, and looking for all the world like the woman who had conquered all.

"I'm not ready for this, Leigh Ann. I may never be ready for this. For a brief moment out there in the hall with Danny, I . . ." Jennifer hung her head. ". . . I reverted."

"What? Don't tell me that slimeball made a move on you. Did he try to kiss you?"

She stared in disbelief at Leigh Ann, who made tiny fists and rose up on her toes, bouncing on the balls of her feet, not unlike the Cowardly Lion. One good swat and she'd go down for the count.

"No kisses. What I mean is that, for a moment, I felt like I was eighteen again."

"See there. Now that's the whole point of these reunions," Leigh Ann assured her, relaxing and patting Jennifer's arm while craning her neck to search the crowd once more. "You need to get out more instead of writing all the time, to be around old friends, to let some of that old fun bubble back up."

"I don't want anything bubbling back up, and I certainly don't want to be eighteen again. Eighteen was not fun for me. I want to go home. There's not a single person here I have any interest in talking with."

"What about Cheri Thomas or Megan Peters? They were your very best friends. The three of you were together so much you looked like Siamese triplets."

"If you haven't noticed, Leigh Ann, they aren't *here*. Cheri is in Panama with the Peace Corps and Megan is a nurse in Atlanta. She doesn't do reunions. So whatever it is that you think—"

"Oh, my," Leigh Ann gasped. "Tell me that isn't who I think it is. Who would have thought he'd have the nerve . . ."

Jennifer turned. Indeed, the crowd had parted, not in respect or awe but perhaps from fear of contamination. Ben Underwood—older, tanned, broad shoulders under his jacket, and hair cut so close to his scalp it might as well have been shaved—had walked in the door.

"I thought he left Macon years ago," Jennifer whispered.

"I think he did," Leigh Ann agreed. "I know if I'd been

charged with murder, I wouldn't be back, especially not to my tenth high school reunion."

"He was never charged with anything," Jennifer reminded her. "He was only questioned."

But as much as she wanted to believe that the police's decision to drop the case had washed away any suspicion of guilt, it hadn't. Only God and Ben Underwood knew if he had anything to do with the disappearance of Jimmy Mitchell.

"He swore he didn't harm Jimmy," Jennifer added. She didn't know if she was trying to convince Leigh Ann or herself.

"And then he clammed up."

"Maybe that's all he had to tell."

"The guy was a punk, Jen, and if the police had found Jimmy's body, they probably would have tried and convicted him of murder."

"It's almost impossible to get a conviction without a body," Jennifer pointed out. "I don't think they even found any evidence of a crime. It was as if Jimmy . . . simply . . . vanished." She shuddered. She had spent more than a few sleepless nights in a room with every light turned on the summer after Jimmy Mitchell had gone missing.

And a few nights over the years since. Just because.

"We're not even supposed to know about it," Jennifer whispered. "Ben was a minor when it happened."

"As if anything that ever happened at Riverside High School could be kept quiet," Leigh Ann said. "The court may have sealed the records, but they couldn't seal the gossip. He gives me the willies. Always did. Even before Jimmy disappeared. He's got those steely gray eyes and he never blinks." She gave a little involuntary shake of her shoulders. "Creeps me out.

"And look at that haircut." She pointed, and Jennifer

quickly caught her finger and pulled it down. "Not to mention those shoulders. Do you think he's been in prison all this time, pumping iron just waiting to get out and show up back here in Macon?"

"Why would he do that?"

"Revenge, of course," Leigh Ann said. "They say psychopaths get a taste for murder. Maybe, after he left Macon, he killed somebody someplace else, only this time the police found the body, and they had enough evidence to convict him, and—"

"Leigh Ann!"

"—and he's come back to do in every one of us who ever whispered behind his back—"

"Would you just cool it? The man has as much right to be here as anybody."

Underwood swaggered over to the refreshment table, and Jennifer watched as a flustered Flo Steiner poured him a glass of punch. He downed the liquid, winced, and handed the glass back to Flo, raising his hand to indicate he only wanted it half full. She watched as he pulled a flask from his jacket pocket, filled the cup the rest of the way, and then swallowed the liquid in one gulp.

"Did you see that?" Leigh Ann declared. "He's drinking."

"No, he's drunk," Jennifer corrected her, registering that his swagger was closer to a stagger.

"Is Jimmy here yet?" he called out to nobody in particular.

Flo's eyes grew huge and she stepped back from the table.

"Jimmy, Jimmy, Jimmy. Where are you, boy? These folks have been waiting for years to see you. You wouldn't want to disappoint them, now would you? Come out, come out, wherever you are."

Involuntarily, Jennifer found herself searching the crowd. Was it possible? Could Jimmy Mitchell actually be there?

A uniformed security guard approached the table and spoke to Ben. He immediately quieted down, and Jennifer watched as the guard confiscated the flask. Then Ben picked up a plastic fork and a plate with a large slab of cake and moved farther back toward the far corner of the room, where Jennifer lost sight of him.

The crowd, finding their manners again, quit gawking and went back to talking, most likely about Ben, if their occasional glances toward the far side of the room were any indication.

"What the heck was that all about?" Leigh Ann asked.

"I have no idea."

"Maybe it's part of his psychopathic behavior. Everybody knows Jimmy's dead. He is dead, isn't he, Jennifer?"

She shrugged. If Leigh Ann had asked her three minutes ago, she would have agreed, but now . . . After all, she'd always secretly hoped that Jimmy had simply run away. If he had . . .

"It's all right, don't you think, that Ben's here?" Leigh Ann added. "I mean, even if he did something to Jimmy, or Lord knows how many other folks, he wouldn't dare try anything, at least not here, not in front of all these people—"

"So what's up, girlfriend?" The voice over Jennifer's shoulder made them both jump. She turned to come face-to-face, actually more like chin-to-nose, with Teri, who, though a little shorter, more than made up with attitude what she lacked in inches.

Teri was another member of their writing group. She wrote romantic suspense and was also unpublished. All they needed now was for April and Monique to show up and they could hold an impromptu critique session, a truly hideous thought.

"You almost gave me a heart attack coming up on me like that," Jennifer declared, putting a hand to her chest.

"Ben Underwood got you spooked, huh?" Teri grinned, white teeth in that sweet cocoa-colored face. Her dark hair, usually straightened, was formed into spiral curls pulled back and up in a cascade, the aqua of her dress complimenting the richness of her brown skin. She didn't look at all like her normal, athletic self. She looked, well, almost angelic.

False advertising. Teri was a lot of things, but angel didn't make the top one hundred.

"You know who Underwood is?" Leigh Ann asked. "I knew the story was all over Riverside High but—"

"Are you kidding me?" Teri interrupted. "Did I not grow up in Macon? Do people not talk in this town? Of course I know about it, even all the way across town. 'You go out late at night and not tell me where you're going, young lady, and you're gonna wind up like that Mitchell boy, where *nobody* can find you.'"

Teri's imitation of her mother was dead-on, right down to the I-have-attitude twist of her neck. "Shoot, my mother got at least six good years of threats out of that one." She shoveled a piece of cake into her mouth and chewed with relish.

"Why are you here?" Jennifer asked, only now registering what's-wrong-with-this-picture. "You didn't go to this school."

"That's right. Our football team kicked your team's—"

Leigh Ann shook her head and then nodded in the direction of one very large man standing nearby who had turned to listen. Jennifer recognized him as a former quarterback.

"Hey, that was years ago. No reason to rehash old rivalries." Teri took another bite of cake. "Leigh Ann called me and told me to get over here, said that you might need a ride home before the night was out."

"Did you have any trouble getting in?" Leigh Ann asked. "Aren't they checking names at the door?"

"I breezed right past those folks. I don't think they even noticed."

Jennifer glowered at Leigh Ann.

"You called her?" she sputtered, finally realizing what Teri had said. "You dragged me to this—this endurance test, because you couldn't bear to come alone, and then you called Teri to come take me home? There was an easy way to eliminate the middleman."

But Leigh Ann wasn't listening. Instead she stood gaping, her chest heaving.

What could possibly be going on now?

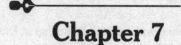

Chapter 7

Jennifer followed Leigh Ann's gaze and squinted at the crowd of sport jackets and party dresses that had gathered near the front entrance of the huge room. "What are you looking—"

Then she saw him, wearing jeans with one knee out and a longsleeve black T-shirt with what looked like the logo for D'Addario Guitars silk-screened across the front. Thin, but still muscular, longish brown hair clipped just below his ears and artificially streaked with blond. Not quite as good-looking as Brad Pitt—didn't have the nose—but definitely cute. Not at all Jennifer's type, but if the look on Leigh Ann's face was any indication, definitely hers.

"Whoa!" Teri said. "Is that who I think it is?"

"Do you two *know* that guy?" Jennifer asked.

Leigh Ann had gone into some kind of shock, her eyes so big and round they seemed to fill her face. That air of confidence she sported, especially where the opposite sex was concerned, had vanished. She looked young, vulnerable, almost shy.

Leigh Ann faced Jennifer, her head down, holding Jennifer's upper arms in a death grip. "Oh, God. I thought he might come, but—"

"Cool it, girl," Teri warned. "Now is no time to show fear."

"I . . . I . . . I . . ." Leigh Ann gulped in air.

"Breathe normally," Jennifer cautioned her.

"He . . . he . . . he . . ."

"Okay, we've got the pronouns down. Would you like to try for a verb?"

Leigh Ann swallowed hard and looked up at Jennifer, her eyes even larger, if that were possible. "What's he doing?"

"Coming this way," Teri told her.

"Hide me," she begged, tightening her grip.

"What—"

"You're absolutely right," Leigh Ann said. "Neither one of us is mature enough to handle something as simple as a high school reunion. You can drive my car, can't you?" She released her grip on Jennifer and fumbled in her purse for her keys, then gave it up. "Teri's got hers. Do you think we can get away before—"

"Hello, Leigh Ann."

Something about the way he said her name made even Jennifer pause. Soft, throaty, passionate. Theirs could not have been a casual relationship.

Leigh Ann froze. Then she squared her shoulders and pulled her bag across her arm. She gave Jennifer a desperate look, mouthed the words *Please don't leave me*, and then pasted on a smile and turned. "Gavin. Well, now, this is a surprise. You know my friend Jennifer, don't you?" Reaching back, she grabbed Jennifer with her talons and dragged her up next to her.

He smiled. Then he slung the hair out of his eyes and offered Jennifer his hand. His touch was sensual, somehow more intimate than she cared to experience. She snatched back her hand, suddenly understanding a whole lot more about Leigh Ann than she ever had before.

And she thought she'd had problems dealing with Danny.

"Gavin Lawless," he said. "I think I was a couple of years behind you. I was in Leigh Ann's class."

"This is Teri," Leigh Ann added, pulling her up on her other side, creating a phalanx.

He nodded and smiled. "Nice to meet you."

"We ... we dated for a while," Leigh Ann confessed. "Only he was Lawson then, not Lawless."

His eyes were sky blue, almost too light to be real.

"I was hoping you'd be here," he said, ducking to catch her gaze, which was darting everywhere about the room, everywhere but in his eyes.

They looked cute together. He was eight or nine inches taller than Leigh Ann's five feet. Their coloring—his light, her dark—made a nice contrast.

"Could you excuse us," he said, gently taking Leigh Ann's hands and pulling her out from between her two friends. She blushed, maybe for the first time in Jennifer's memory, and let him lead her away.

Which left Jennifer in that intolerable friend limbo trying to figure out exactly what it was that Leigh Ann—assuming she herself knew—wanted her to do: make a scene and snatch her back, or let her go.

"So what's going on with those two?" Teri asked, pointing.

"Something powerful," Jennifer said.

They watched as Leigh Ann and Gavin disappeared into the crowd, leaving Jennifer shaking her head.

"She called you?" Jennifer asked, turning to face Teri.

"Yep. 'Bout forty minutes ago. Told me to get over here pronto because she was afraid you might not last the night. She said she had some unfinished business to take care of, which, apparently, she is in the middle of handling even as we speak. She said she didn't want to leave you stranded if you decided you couldn't hack memory lane. So, that's Gavin."

"You know about him?" Jennifer asked.

"So do you. You know that alpha male Leigh Ann is so fond of writing about in her romance novels?"

"The charismatic rebel who leaves a string of broken hearts and promises before the heroine finally finds his heart of gold?"

"That's the man. Seems he lives and breathes among us. At least for tonight."

"Exactly how is it that you know all this and I don't?" Jennifer asked, more than a little peeved. Leigh Ann and Teri were always fussing at each other. It hurt that Leigh Ann would choose to confide in Teri and not in her.

"She didn't think you'd approve."

"Are you saying they still have a relationship?"

"No. He had some problems."

"What kind of problems?"

Teri shrugged. "They haven't seen each other since they graduated. He took the first bus out of Macon. He's a musician. From somewhere out West. California, I think."

"Successful?"

"On his way. He's got two CDs on the market with a third coming out fairly soon from some obscure label. Guitar music, part of the folk resurgence. There was a piece in the style section of yesterday's paper about him."

"But why would he go all the way to California if he wanted to be a musician? Little Richard, James Brown, Otis Redding, the Allman Brothers—they all came out of Macon. Phoenix Sound Recording Studios is right downtown."

"True, but they're not exactly folk icons."

"Don't give me that. Red Fish, Blu Fish got their start here, too."

"Okay, okay." Teri rolled her eyes. "Maybe he thought

the soul influence was too strong for what he wanted to do. Don't ask me. I've never met the guy before. Anyway, Leigh Ann says he bummed around Nashville for a while and then made his way further out. But he's back in town for a couple of weeks talking to some people here, probably down at Phoenix. He dropped her a postcard saying if he could possibly make time, he'd look her up."

"A postcard?"

"Like I said, a real alpha male."

"But why would he bother? I don't mean about looking up Leigh Ann, but about coming to the reunion? I vaguely remember him. He was a quiet, scrawny little kid. Kept to himself. Definitely not one of the in-crowd."

Teri shrugged. "Don't tell me that if you had a CD to promote, you wouldn't be back home spreading the word." She scraped at her paper plate and savored the last bit of butter cream icing.

Teri wiped her mouth with a napkin and gave her another one of her looks. "I know that if—that is, *when*—I sell a book I want everyone in my high school class to know it. I might just have to take out a big ad in the *Telegraph*."

"You're scary," Jennifer told her. She could honestly say—with the possible exception of Sheena Cassidy—she had nothing to prove to anybody from Riverside High. Except maybe Mrs. Ledbetter, the English teacher who, she would say, never shared her sense of humor. And maybe Jordan Watson, that intolerable geek in computer class who kept slipping programs on her machine that made the letters fall off the screen as she typed them. And that guy in gym class with the aerosol can of whipped cream. And . . . Okay. Maybe Teri had a point.

"So what do we do?" Jennifer said. "She asked me not to leave."

"Classic conflicting behavior. I say we stick around and

see what happens. Besides, I've seen worse parties, and I did spy one mmm-mmm good-lookin' brother in black near the far bleachers. . . ." Now it was Teri's turn to crane her neck and search the crowd.

"So what am I supposed to do while you're macking on this Campbell soup guy?"

"Chill out. Circulate. Enjoy life, something you could use some practice doing. Could be one of those little geeks you went to school with came of age."

Jennifer sighed and took a quick look around the room. There had to be somebody there she wouldn't mind talking to. If she couldn't find them, it was going to be a long night, because the one thing she knew she couldn't do was desert Leigh Ann.

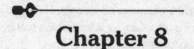

Chapter 8

Leigh Ann and Gavin had dropped off the face of the earth. So had Danny. Not that Jennifer was looking for him. At least not with any real effort. She had long since lost Teri to a group, the one with the guy all in black, who was currently hassling the deejay, most likely about not playing enough R&B.

About fifteen minutes ago she'd stuck her head out the door and checked the parking lot. Leigh Ann's car was still there. Unless they'd skipped out in Gavin's, they had to be around somewhere.

Ben Underwood had also dropped out of sight, not that she was consciously keeping tabs on him, at least not that she'd admit even to herself. Too bad she didn't know what kind of car he drove.

And, of course, Jimmy Mitchell had failed to show.

She thought she'd caught a glimpse of Teague McAfee, one of her most unfavorite people. But why would one of the hungriest reporters for the *Atlanta Eye*, the state's sleaziest tabloid, show up at *her* high school reunion? She had to have been mistaken.

"So what's the deal? Why won't they buy your books?" Seth Yarborough asked, popping a handful of pastel-colored butter mints into his mouth. "Don't book publishers have any taste?"

He grinned at her with his young, good-looking, tousle-headed boy smile, which made her remember why Seth had been such a big man on campus. He was the only other one of Danny's group to ever take any interest in her.

His charm had a character all its own. He made everyone feel worthy of his attention, as if he saw the real person, the one other teenagers ignored.

But that attention had its limits. As soon as Seth turned his head, as soon as a person was out of his field of vision, his focus shifted to someone else, and it was as though he'd never known whomever he'd been so intent on just minutes before. That's why Jennifer didn't trust him even if he was an assistant district attorney, and why she found it so strange that he'd sought her out tonight, that he actually seemed to remember who she was.

"My books will sell," she said, sounding more confident than she felt at the moment.

"You married?" he asked, looking down at her. He was tall, blond, and still slender, and wore his tailored suit like he was comfortable in it. He must be many a woman's dream, she thought. He'd certainly been a lot of girls'.

"Nope. You?"

"Just finished with number three."

Must be that field-of-vision problem.

"Danny Buckner was looking for you earlier," he said casually, and then looked her in the eyes. "Did he find you?"

She nodded. "I talked to him for just a moment."

"He was nuts about you in high school," he said, shoveling the last of the mints into his mouth.

That comment made her pause. She hardly expected anyone other than Danny, Sheena, and herself to remember that she and Danny had ever dated.

Before she could think of a clever response, he grabbed

her hand and gave it a squeeze. "Gotta go. They're giving me a signal. Maybe I'll give you a call."

A call? Jennifer stifled the laugh bubbling in her throat. Maybe she was further from high school than she'd thought. There was a time when she would have given a lot to have Seth Yarborough give her a call, just so she could tell her girlfriends about it. Those days were long gone.

She watched as Seth bounded up on stage and took the mike. Maybe something interesting would finally happen. This night had turned into its own special kind of never-ending hell.

"All right, gang, this is it, so listen up," he said. While waiting a moment for the talking to die down, he stood there bouncing with all the energy of the member-of-every-club sort of guy she remembered him being. It made her tired just to watch him.

"In my capacity as one of your senior class presidents," he began, "one who graduated—it's hard for me to believe—twelve years ago, I'd like to welcome all of you, no matter when you graduated, back to Riverside High."

The crowd cheered and clapped.

Seth Yarborough bobbed his head at them and grinned with that friendly aw-shucks attitude that made everybody like him whether they wanted to or not. "Unfortunately, Gwen Hollen, president of the class celebrating its tenth reunion, couldn't make it this year. She's in England on her honeymoon. She sends her regards. But if you're disappointed Gwen couldn't be here, we've got a really special treat for you. Gavin Lawless is with us."

He paused dramatically, as though waiting for the room to explode into applause. "Okay. So you don't know his name yet, but you will soon. He's one of the rising stars on the folk circuit. I got a promo of a single from his next, soon-to-be-released CD in the mail, and I can guarantee that he's going to be the next big name on the folk charts." He looked down as though speaking directly to someone at the foot of the platform. "They do have charts for folk music, don't they?" He grinned, looking back up and out over the crowd. "So, Gavin, how about coming up and giving us a sample?"

He waited for several seconds, but nothing happened. No one stirred. "I know he's here. I saw him come in. Anybody know where he is?"

Someone in the back hollered, "Who the hell cares?" and the group broke up with laughter as Yarborough's face flushed.

"Okay then. Why don't we just get on with the evening's festivities. Personally, I've always felt that if you had the good luck to make it through prom unscathed, you shouldn't push it. Unfortunately, the planning committee didn't ask my opinion, so here goes."

He pulled out an index card and read from it. "It's my pleasure to once again introduce your court and your king and queen of ten years ago, an echo from your past of what truly must have been a Night to Remember."

Jennifer felt stunned, like she'd been hit upside the head. This was a room full of seemingly mature adults. Had they all lost their minds?

A woman passed by and thrust a small plastic bag filled with confetti into Jennifer's hands. Watching was one thing, participating quite another. Numbly, she handed it to the woman next to her who seemed delighted to have two.

The crowd parted and there she was. Sheena Cassidy Buckner, queen for a day, beaming as if she'd just been crowned Miss America.

The simple truth hit Jennifer in one brilliant revelation: Sheena Cassidy Buckner had peaked in high school, when she'd been named prom queen. Why else would she try to re-create that glory?

Sheena brushed by with her escort, a rather handsome fellow who apparently was that year's king and who made Jennifer wonder where he'd been hiding when she was in school. They made their way across the floor, through waves of confetti, and up onto the stage.

Sheena came complete with crown, sash, long-stemmed red rose to match her dress, lips, and fingernails, and a million-dollar smile.

The crowd clapped politely—wondering, as she was, Jennifer suspected, exactly where all this was going and why they were going there.

"So, Gary, do you have a few words to say to the crowd?" Yarborough asked.

The king, sans crown or sash or any other outward sign of his regal status, shook his head and stepped back, his neck coloring just enough to indicate his true feelings.

"Sheena?"

She took the mike, grinned, and took a deep breath. Before she could get a word out, a tall woman with dark, bobbed hair broke from the court behind and went after Sheena, grabbing the crown with one hand and the mike with the other, bobby pins flying every which way.

"You scheming witch. I was robbed," the woman yelled. "Ten years I've waited for this, you—you—"

The two swayed back and forth like a push-me-pull-me toy as flashes from a camera went off and Jennifer, as well as everyone around her, stood frozen in horror. The other woman, who obviously hadn't peaked in high school, apparently had wanted to.

"You counted the votes. A candidate can't count the votes," the woman gasped out between gritted teeth, forcing

Sheena backward, her back arching dangerously toward the edge of the stage.

Sheena let go of the mike and soared forward, grabbing a handful of her opponent's hair, yanking hard, but never once losing her grip on the treasured crown.

The other woman went down squealing. The brunette's escort, who had at last recovered from his paralysis, managed to ram his body between the two women and drag the sobbing brunette away.

Jennifer winced. This was too painful to watch. Jerry Springer had come to Riverside High.

She hoped the woman wouldn't tear back on stage, her eyes glowing a dangerous red. All they needed to make the evening even more interesting was a Southern version of *Carrie*.

Sheena brushed dark hair from her hand, regained the mike, adjusted her crown and her sash, and addressed the crowd.

"I'm so sorry you all had to see that. Obviously, Mary Jo has never gotten over being first runner-up for the honor I so proudly bear, your Miss Riverside High School. It is truly delightful to be among you tonight. As chairman of the planning committee, I hope each of you is having the most wonderful time. I'd like to take just a few minutes to thank the people in my life who—"

Yarborough snatched the mike away. "Thank *you*, Sheena. Now I'd like to take you back, back to that night however many years ago when you were eighteen, love was sweet, life was simple"—he threw a pointed look at Sheena, who appeared ready to take him on like she had Mary Jo—"and the biggest question on your mind was will she or won't she. Find that special gal or guy of yours. It's slow-dance time."

Yarborough replaced the mike in its stand and pointed at the deejay. Strains of "The Time of My Life" filled the air.

The group on stage broke up as spouses joined members of the court, and couples made their way to the gym floor.

But something was wrong.

Left alone at the edge of the stage, Sheena had dropped her rose and, shading her eyes with one hand, peered out, searching the crowd. Where *was* Danny Buckner?

Something seemed to catch Sheena's eye. She turned toward the main doors, and so did Jennifer.

Al Carpenter had just come in from outside, his face grave, and he was beckoning to her. Sheena hurried down the steps, holding her crown in place with one hand, and made her way through the crowd.

Jennifer watched as Carpenter tried to pull Sheena toward the door. She struggled out of his grip, her lips moving rapidly, as if spitting out words, her face no longer pretty. Al placed one hand on each of Sheena's shoulders, shook his head, and then spoke to her. She crumpled, Al catching her in his arms before she hit the floor. Then she threw back her head and let out a wail that rang above the music and through the room like a banshee's cry. A shiver went straight to Jennifer's soul.

The crown fell from Sheena's head and rolled across the floor.

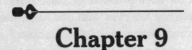

Chapter 9

"Danny can't be ..." Jennifer couldn't bring herself to say the word, as she clutched the lapels of Sam's jacket.

"Dead?" Sam supplied, one hand resting on her hip, the other holding a large Dunkin' Donuts coffee.

She pulled back, suddenly not wanting to be associated with someone, even Sam, for whom that word came quite that easily.

"Are they sure it was him? Maybe they made a mistake," she insisted, again grabbing his lapels and splashing the coffee. Maybe if she argued long and hard enough with Sam she might be able to bully him into changing what had happened.

"I don't think so. His wife made a positive ID," Sam assured her, pulling a napkin from his pocket and mopping up the coffee that had spilled down the side of the container. He handed Teri the cup and put his arm around Jennifer.

"Sheena. She must be devastated," Jennifer said. She couldn't help but feel sorry for Danny's widow, even if she was Sheena. "Where is she?"

"Talking to the police, I'm sure. You're shivering," he told her. "Let me give you my coat." He let go of her and started to pull off his jacket, but she pulled it back into place.

"No, I'm fine. Really," she insisted, patting his chest.

Teri came up beside her, linked arms, and gently tugged. "You need to sit, my friend." She pulled her down onto the bleachers, but Jennifer bounced right back up.

"Sam, how long has he been . . . gone?" Jennifer asked, managing, somehow, to get at least that word out of her mouth. She was too numb to feel grief, but not too numb to feel guilt. She'd let Danny walk away from her earlier that evening and he had died. Maybe if she'd made him stay with her . . .

"They're saying an hour, maybe more," Sam told her. "It probably happened shortly after the reunion began." He'd lost his professional distance. He seemed concerned, his face solemn, not because of what had happened but because of her reaction to it.

He tugged her down next to him as he sat.

She reached for Teri's hand and clutched it in a death grip. She only wished she knew where Leigh Ann had gotten off to. She wanted all of her friends safe and accounted for.

Gently, Sam leaned over, tipping her chin up and staring at her with those deep, dark blue eyes of his, the ones that were the well of truth. "Just how well did you know this guy?"

She winced and dropped her gaze, swiping at the water gathering in her eyes. "Long time ago. We . . . were friends."

Teri made a kind of choking sound, and Jennifer elbowed her.

Whatever Sam thought, he let it pass.

For several moments they sat there, no one talking, Jennifer staring out at the gym floor. Sam took back his coffee from Teri and sipped it, his arm still circling Jennifer's shoulders. She knew she should have found it comforting, having him that close, but somehow all she felt was confused.

"I know this is hard for you," he said gently. "When someone you grew up with dies—"

"That's not what this is about," she snapped at him, shrugging out of his embrace. She had all kinds of trouble dealing with mortality, her own as well as everyone else's, but what Sam was saying was only part of it. She touched his arm. "I'm sorry. It's just that Danny had a problem. He needed help." And she hadn't given it to him.

"What kind of problem?" He took her hand, lacing his fingers with her own.

She jerked back, her fingers stinging from a twelve-year-old memory.

"Sorry," she repeated sheepishly. "I can't do anything right tonight." It'd help if she could get herself under control. Danny had pulled her over the line, back into the past, and then he'd gone and died on her, leaving her half here and half there. Where was that maturity she'd struggled so hard to develop?

"I want to go home," she announced.

"You can't. Not until the police have questioned everybody," Sam told her.

Teri leaned across in front of Jennifer. "What are you doing here?" she asked Sam. "Don't they let you off work even for one evening?"

Quietly, Sam explained that he'd picked up the police call off the scanner and gotten over to the school as soon as he realized they were talking about the reunion. He'd assessed the situation outside as quickly as he could, made some notes, and then waded through the crowd to find Jennifer.

"Can I get the two of you anything while we wait? Maybe a cold drink?" he offered.

Jennifer shook her head. At this point she didn't want anything except to relive the last two hours, to handle things differently, to insist that Danny tell her what was wrong, to keep him from going out to his car and . . .

God. How could this happen? Danny Buckner was her age. *Her* age. People weren't supposed to die that young, especially not someone she'd once cared about. Especially not Danny.

Teri hugged her shoulders. "Hey, sweetie, it had to have been an accident," she said. "It sucks, but accidents like that happen all the time. You get a hole in your muffler and you sit there with the motor running and your windows up and all that carbon monoxide building up—"

"Why would you sit in your car with the motor running on a spring night?" Jennifer demanded.

"Air-conditioning, maybe?" Teri suggested.

"They're saying suicide," Sam said. "A piece of hose was stuffed into the tailpipe, the other end into the driver's side window. Some kind of T-shirt or cloth was found wedged between the glass and the door frame to make a seal. His skin was flushed a bright red. I think they're right on target with this one."

"Jesus, Mary, and Joseph," Teri volunteered. "How could someone not notice a car running like that?"

"Someone did," Sam said, "just not soon enough. Some guy had come by to pick up his wife, took a swing around the lot looking for a space, but nothing was open. So he pulled around to the side of the building, behind a car parked in a no-parking zone near the service ramp. He noticed the car was running and got out to ask if the driver was leaving."

Danny had died in his favorite parking place.

Her stomach lurched, and she stuffed her free hand, which had begun to shake, under her thigh. Her ears rang and she felt a little dizzy. Suicide. How could he? She thought he had more courage than that.

"He'd obviously been there awhile," Sam added. "Not much activity in the lot. Most everyone was in here having a good time."

Jennifer shot him a glance. Not everyone.

"Besides, no one would think too much about some guy sitting in a car like that, and the sound of the motor in these new cars is low-key."

"How could he kill himself?" Jennifer blurted out. "Why would Danny do that? Why would—"

She stopped when she heard her name, and turned to look up into Seth Yarborough's grave face.

"How you doin'?" he asked, touching her hand.

She shook her head, suddenly unable to speak. Seth had been Danny's friend, too.

"Seth" was all she could say. She let go of Teri, stood and hugged him to her, the tears she'd tried so hard to keep back now flowing freely. She pulled back, suddenly embarrassed. She and Seth had never been more than acquaintances. He offered her his handkerchief. She used it to wipe her face.

"I know," he said. "If you need to talk, you call me at the courthouse. Any time. You hear me? Or at home. The police will be speaking with you, but you may feel more comfortable with someone you know." He pressed his card into her hand. "Tell you what, I'll give you a ring sometime tomorrow and—"

"There she is!" It was as if Sheena had appeared out of nowhere, a policeman on either side, shrieking like one of the pod-people unmasking a human in *Invasion of the Body Snatchers*.

Seth squeezed her hand and pulled back. "Tomorrow" was all he said before disappearing into the crowd, leaving Sheena shrieking.

Jennifer looked behind her, hoping beyond hope that Sheena was pointing at someone else.

"She knows," Sheena said with absolute certainty.

A policewoman approached.

Sam was immediately on his feet. "What's this all about?"

"Are you Jennifer Marsh?" the officer asked.

Jennifer nodded. "But I don't—"

"Come with me, please." The woman gently directed her by the shoulder.

"You can't—" Sam began.

"We simply want to ask her a few questions," the policewoman assured him. "I'll have her back in a few minutes."

Jennifer felt panic prickle through her body, which, having ditched the fight option, was poised for flight. She glanced desperately toward Sam and Teri, but all she got in return were two shrugs.

"We'll wait," Sam assured her.

Now that was helpful.

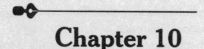

Chapter 10

"That . . . that . . ." Jennifer repeated as she paced.

"I don't know why you're having trouble finding the word," Teri said. "I can think of half a dozen. You want I should start alphabetically with the Bs?"

"She actually told them I knew all about Danny and what was eating at him. Then she had the nerve to tell the police that I was the last person to see him alive. As if that wasn't enough, she brought up everything that happened twelve years ago and accused me of stealing him away from her."

"Now that's a bad one. What's it carry? Twenty to life?" Teri yawned and rubbed both her eyes.

"Ooooh. I could . . . I could . . ." Twelve years of repressed and not-so-repressed anger bubbled to the surface.

"Capture that thought and see if you can't get it into that chapter you showed us last week. That's what I was trying to tell you was missing, that seething hatred."

Sensing the knotted muscles in her neck, Jennifer stopped and uncurled her fists. Hatred? Did she *hate* Sheena? She thought she'd forgiven Sheena years ago. Looked like she had some work of her own to do. "It's just that the police were treating me like I was Dr. Kervorkian, like I helped him kill himself."

What's more, before she'd left the high school, she had to explain to Sam about her relationship with Danny. And about Sheena. And Danny trying to talk to her that night. All of which she'd hoped to never have to mention to anybody ever again, least of all Sam.

She started pacing again.

"Do you mind? You're wearing a groove in my mom's new carpet," Teri said, trying to prop open her eyelids with her fingers. "Besides, it's—" She checked her watch. "Holy ... Do you know it's almost three-thirty in the morning? Calm down."

But she couldn't calm down. Danny was dead, Sheena was still causing her grief after all these years, and something was very, very wrong.

Teri's eyes, heavily lined and shadowed with the same aqua as her dress, drifted shut, and she tumbled sideways against the arm of the chocolate-brown corduroy couch. She jerked back up and put her index finger to her lips. "Shhhh. You'll wake my mom."

"Your mom takes her hearing aid out before she goes to sleep."

"Okay, then, you'll wake me."

"It was your idea to bring me home with you, all the way across Macon to the south side," Jennifer reminded her.

After her confession, she'd sent Sam off to write up the story for the *Telegraph*. He'd only agreed to go when Teri assured him she would see to Jennifer. What was worse, he'd been so unbearably nice about it all.

Teri had bundled her into the car and taken her home like a lost cat. She'd cut the headlights, using only the glow of the streetlamp to see, when they pulled into the driveway of the modest one-story brick house two blocks off Pio Nono. Her mom's bedroom was at the far left front corner, and Teri didn't want to wake her with the flash of headlights. She'd maneuvered the car between the two large magnolia trees growing out of the packed red clay, and parked in front of the carport.

Teri had grown up there. She told everyone she stayed because she couldn't afford a place of her own, but Jennifer suspected it was because her mom was alone.

"If I'd had my car with me, I wouldn't be here," Jennifer informed her. "I asked you to take me to my apartment. I felt awful calling Mrs. Ramon so late and asking her to walk Muffy one last time for the evening."

"I didn't want you staying by yourself tonight, fretting. I thought if you came here you might get some sleep. Silly me. I can't even get you to sit." Teri reached over and pulled Jennifer down next to her onto the sofa. "Muffy obeys better than you do."

"They didn't find a suicide note," Jennifer reminded her.

"We've been all over this more times than I can count. Besides, most suicides don't leave notes."

"You made that up."

"Yeah, but it sounds right. Face it, Jen. The guy had a problem, a big problem. If his wife is half of what you say she is, I'm surprised he survived this long." She yawned broadly, snuggled her head against Jennifer's shoulder and closed her eyes. "Besides, he's her concern. You were done with him long ago. I don't know why you're worrying about his problems now. He certainly isn't."

Teri had a point. Jennifer lived with an overactive conscience, and if there was blame to go around, she always seemed first in line.

Still, Danny had come to her asking for help, or at least she felt sure he would have if it hadn't been for Al Carpenter. And she had done nothing. What if this time when Carpenter showed up, she'd told him to take a hike? What if she could have made a difference in whether or not Danny died?

Abruptly, she stood up, and Teri plopped sideways onto the sofa cushion. "You can't tell me that a person would choose such a public place to commit suicide. It doesn't make any sense. He would have gone home where he could have a nice garage—assuming he had a garage—to poison himself in. The chances of someone finding him in that parking lot—"

"But no one found him, Jen. He wasn't actually in the lot. Besides, everyone was inside." Teri shook her head. "People who take their own lives are irrational, backed into some kind of corner. If they weren't, they wouldn't do it. But he did."

But Danny hadn't seemed at all irrational when she spoke with him earlier. Nor had he been one to avoid problems—except where Sheena was concerned. He'd been at the reunion. With friends. It simply didn't make any sense.

"If it was suicide, that's between Danny and God. But what if it wasn't. What if it was—"

"Oh, no," Teri groaned. "Don't even go there. He killed himself, Jen, and you're just going to have to accept it."

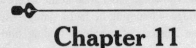

Chapter 11

The answering machine was flashing when Jennifer got home close to one o'clock Sunday afternoon. She'd awakened around noon, and Teri's mom had forced her to eat some cheese grits when she politely refused the fried chicken (the one food on earth that threatened her vegetarianism), milk gravy (okay, that, too), homemade biscuits, mashed potatoes, and collard greens that Mona had prepared when she got back from church. She'd muttered something about Jennifer wasting away to nothing from a protein deficiency, and poured her an enormous glass of whole milk to go with it. Mona's concept of the ideal weight was a good deal higher than that of the general public.

The grits, comfort food of the highest order, were pretty darn good, and she was indeed hungrier than she thought. Mona stood guard until every last bite of grits and every last sip of milk had disappeared. Then she allowed Teri to drive her home. Jennifer missed having a mama of her own, so she didn't at all mind having Mona fill in on occasion, especially when she was tired and confused.

She shoved the door of her apartment closed behind her, dumped her purse on the table, and turned to pick up a slip of paper lying on the floor just inside the door. Sam. He'd been by to check on her. The note said he hoped she was feeling better and that he'd stop by later, after she'd had a chance to rest. Sweet.

Her head hurt in that deep place behind her right eye. Wasn't it enough that she was emotionally drained? Did her body have to turn on her, too?

Muffy was pulling her you-abandoned-me act by pretending not to have heard her come in, which was just fine with Jennifer. Fortunately, Mrs. Ramon had volunteered to take her out in the morning, too. A human ego held no candle to a dog's.

She hit the Play button on the answering machine, and the tone screeched at her. Why the heck did they make those things so loud?

"Jennifer, you know and I know they're wrong. Danny didn't kill himself. Jennifer, are you there? Pick up. I need to talk to you. Two thirty-six A.M."

Sheena. Why was she calling her? And why was *she* so certain Danny hadn't committed suicide? Of course. Sheena must be carrying some of the same guilt that she herself had been feeling, only multiplied by ten years of marriage. Sheena was at the reunion, too, and certainly knew Danny a whole lot better than she did.

Beeep!

"Jennifer, the police are still saying suicide. They won't listen to me. Why didn't you tell them the truth? Three forty-seven A.M."

Beeep!

"I don't know who else to call."

Sheena's words were slower and softer, barely audible. Jennifer thought she could detect a deep sob of exhaustion in her voice.

"I can't get hold of Al Carpenter. I don't care what you told the police, you've got to tell me what Danny told you last night. Five fifty-three A.M."

Beeep!

"Sorry I didn't catch you in. It's Seth, just calling to check up on you. I'll try you again later. Hope you're getting some rest. Nine forty-two A.M."

So Seth had called. Somehow she'd thought he wouldn't.

Beeep!

"Hey, pretty lady. Understand you were at the Riverside High School reunion Saturday night when one Danny Buckner met his Maker. If I'd known you were there, I would have made it a point to find you. Give me a call, Marsh, and we'll talk. Could be worth dinner to you. With me. What more could a girl ask? See you later. I promise. Ten twenty-seven A.M."

Just the sound of Teague McAfee's voice was enough to make her skin crawl. So he *had* been there last night. Well, he was crazy if he thought she'd let him quote her in the weekly gossip rag, the *Atlanta Eye,* that he wrote for. But young Teague did have a sense of humor, especially if he thought she'd ever call him back. Still, he could be dangerous. If he caught a whiff that she or Sheena suspected that Danny's death might not be suicide, all heck would break loose.

The caller ID showed one unavailable plus three other calls from D. Buckner. Persistent little devil. Like a deer tick. She could cause an irritation, then a rash, and show up later with all kinds of debilitating side effects.

Jennifer sighed. She really ought to call Sheena back. The woman sounded frantic. She lifted the receiver and punched in the first three digits of the number displayed on the caller ID, then stopped and dropped it back into the cradle. Nope. She wasn't going to do it. She didn't owe Sheena a thing. Sheena had been terrible to her not because of anything she'd ever done, but because some boy had liked her. What kind of sense did that make? Sheena's problem had been with Danny, not her, and she didn't care to ever speak to someone who couldn't figure out that simple truth. Even someone obviously in as much pain as Sheena was now. That woman had brought unbelievable grief to her young self and she was still doing it, by siccing the police on her. It'd be a cold day before she sought out Sheena Cassidy Buckner.

Jennifer took two aspirins, wet a washcloth with cold water, kicked off her shoes, and lay down on the couch, draping the rag over her eyes. She wanted all thoughts of Sheena, Teague, and Danny's death out of her head, at least long enough to take a nap. She desperately needed a shower, but it would have to wait, unless she didn't mind falling asleep under running water. Exhaustion rapidly won out, and she sank into the soft oblivion of the weary.

It took her a full minute to realize the pounding that was stirring her consciousness was coming from the door and not from inside her head.

Clutching the cloth to her forehead, she scurried to the door in her stocking feet, blocked a yelping Muffy with her knee, threw back the security bar, and jerked it open. This had better be good.

Without so much as a hello, Sheena, clad in jeans and a T-shirt, a stuffed book bag slung over her shoulder, bumped past her. "Ever hear of returning a phone call?"

Twelve years had done nothing to soften the woman's manner.

But twelve years had done a lot for Jennifer. "Out!" she barked. "Out! Now!" As soon as the words passed her lips, she was sorry. The woman *had* just lost her husband.

Sheena drew back. "What the hell's got into you? All I want is to talk to you."

Muffy growled softly, refusing to leave Jennifer's side

until she gave her a good rub and assured her everything was all right.

Sheena looked her up and down. "God. Don't you have anything else to wear besides that blue jersey?"

She should have changed her clothes. And taken that shower. But how dare Sheena point that out!

"You've got three seconds," Jennifer told her, looking at her watch. Widow or no, she didn't have to put up with insults.

"Danny was murdered," Sheena said.

"So you've been telling my machine. I don't know anything about it, and I certainly don't intend to let you accuse me of—"

"Of what?" Sheena said, staring at her as if she were crazy. "You think that's why I came here, to accuse you of murdering Danny? You're nuttier than even *I* thought you were."

Okay. So maybe even Sheena wouldn't sink that low.

"I don't know why you're here," Jennifer said. "I can't imagine where you got the idea that Danny was murdered." Unless it was from the same place she had gotten hers. "Something was bothering him. You're his wife. What was it? What did he tell you last night?"

"He told me nothing. He said he didn't want to worry me." Sheena's lip curled up in one of those ironic smiles. For a moment Jennifer felt sorry for her. It dawned on her that Sheena was fighting hard not to grieve, that she was running one step ahead of ruination, that if she paused to rest for even a moment, it'd catch her.

"Look. I wouldn't be here if I didn't have to be," Sheena went on. "I don't relish associating with you any more than you do with me. My husband is lying dead in the morgue, and they won't even release his body for burial until they've done an autopsy and finished their investigation. They're saying suicide, and I know it wasn't. And you, whether you'll admit it or not, know it, too. What did he say to you when the two of you went out into the hall together?"

"Nothing. Al Carpenter dragged him away. The only thing he mentioned was in the note I got in the mail. I think he wanted to hire a private investigator. Why?"

Sheena gave her one of her you're-so-dumb looks. "I don't know. Haven't you been listening?"

"Carpenter's an attorney," Jennifer pushed. "He'd have contacts with P.I.'s. So why would Danny be asking me for a recommendation?"

It was a good question, Jennifer thought. One that said something about Danny and Al's relationship. Or one that said something about the nature of what Danny wanted investigated.

But Sheena didn't seem to appreciate her contribution. She acted as if it wasn't worth responding to. She sat down on the floor in front of the couch and pulled her backpack into her lap, unzipping it. She dug out two cans of RC Cola, a box of Ho Hos, and a stack of yearbooks. She popped the top on one of the cans and set the other one toward Jennifer, who had sat down, too.

"So, Jenny. This is where you live. Twelve years out and you're still in some dinky apartment? What you got here? One bedroom?" Sheena took a big swig of cola, fingering the worn fabric of the sofa cushion she was leaning against.

Jennifer wondered if such remarks were sufficient provocation for justifiable homicide. They would be if she were on the jury. She knew calling her Jenny was.

"Talk to Al Carpenter," Jennifer snapped at her. "And the name is Jennifer, not Jenny."

"I can't find Al. His wife, Candy—do you know Candy?"

Jennifer shook her head.

"She was on my cheerleading squad. Did incredible splits. We put her at the top of our pyramids because she was so little. She said Al hasn't been home since before the reunion. She didn't go."

"Did she report it to the police?"

"Nope. Al does that sometimes. Goes out drinking with his buddies. When I find him, we'll talk. Until then, you're it."

Lucky her. "But why me?"

"Whatever it was that had Danny all in a tizzy must have happened about the time the two of you were dating. Why else do you think he was so hot to talk to you?"

That one made her blush and angry, both at herself and at Sheena. What could she say to a question like that?

"We only dated for two weeks," Jennifer reminded her.

"Fifteen and a half days."

Sheeesh. And she thought she was obsessive! "So what was it?" Jennifer demanded.

"I don't know." Sheena tossed a yearbook in Jennifer's direction.

"What do you expect to find in these?"

"For four years this was Danny's world. The people he associated with are all in these books, from students to teachers to staff. Even the janitors. There has to be a picture of someone or something that will jog your memory."

"Don't put this all on me," Jennifer warned. "I don't think I ever really knew Danny."

"You think I did? Talking wasn't something we did a lot of when we were together, especially when we were in high school. Look, Jennifer, I know you don't like this any better than I do, but you're all I've got. I'm not giving you a choice. You know something, all right. You just don't know you know it, and you're going to help me find out what that something is."

Sheena opened Danny's senior yearbook and leafed through it. "Danny hung pretty tight with his crowd. They were one of the most popular groups in school," she said proudly, as though it still mattered.

It had never mattered to Jennifer.

"So, remind me. Who was in the group?" Jennifer asked. She felt certain she knew all their names, that, indeed, she'd seen them all together at the reunion. But perceptions were tricky. It would be best if she let Sheena define Danny's friends.

"Danny and Al, of course. Seth Yarborough and Mick Farmer. They were the main ones."

Sheena flipped the pages until she found Carpenter's senior picture. He had the same shaggy brown hair and football shoulders Jennifer remembered from prom night. In the photo he seemed uncomfortable, confined by his black jacket, white shirt and tie. When she'd seen him last night, his hair had been closely cropped and the football muscle had gone soft to become an early version of middle-age spread.

"He was football captain," Sheena added.

"He didn't go to the prom that year," Jennifer said, more to herself than to Sheena.

"He and Candy were having problems," Sheena said.

"What kind of problems?"

"Who cares? Obviously they worked it out."

Sheena shuffled through to the last page of the senior pictures and tapped her finger at Seth Yarborough. "Senior class president. Math club. Honor society. He went on to Tulane to study law. He currently works as an assistant D.A."

"He makes the newspaper periodically."

"Talk is he may go into politics," Sheena added.

Sheena started to close the book, but Jennifer took it

from her and flipped to the Fs. "You're forgetting Mick Farmer."

"Danny and Mick are in business together."

She noted Sheena's use of the present tense.

"I thought Danny had gone into his dad's business."

"The paint store?" Sheena shook her head. "Only for a year, until he could get enough money together to go out on his own. They do video postproduction work."

"Define that for me."

"How should I know? I think it has something to do with fiddling around with videos that companies make. They edit them, maybe work on the sound, the titles, credits. Heck, I don't know."

"Who had the idea for the business?" Jennifer asked.

"Mick. He got a degree in graphic design from Georgia Tech."

In high school Mick had been part of the group because of Danny. He'd seemed more of the loner type. Seth and Al accepted him only because he and Danny were a package deal.

And Mick always had a thing for Sheena. He took her to the prom that year.

"He had an edge to him," Jennifer observed. She remembered his dark, brooding, tortured-artist allure. Smart. Misunderstood. The perfect project for some girl looking for someone to save, he'd been the one guy all the girls wanted but nobody could get. Even better, he seemed entirely oblivious to his attractiveness.

During the brief time Jennifer and Danny had dated, Sheena used Mick to make Danny jealous. Only it didn't work, and she'd dropped him flat when Danny came back to her.

Jennifer let her finger trace his features and wondered if Sheena had ever been an issue between the two friends.

"This is all fine and good," she said, shutting the yearbook, "but I don't see that it's getting us anywhere. Something must have happened recently to bring Danny's problems to a head, whether he killed himself or, as you seem to think, someone murdered him. What was it?"

Sheena shook her head. "You're not listening to me, Jenny. I don't know why he's been so upset—"

"Think," Jennifer ordered. "Were he and Mick having problems with the business?"

"I don't believe so, but Danny never talked to me about it."

"Not at all?"

"Hardly. I wasn't all that interested." Sheena stacked the yearbooks into a pile and shoved them over to the end of the couch. "I'll leave those here. Maybe if you go through them again . . ."

How could she get through to the woman? "Sure, whatever," Jennifer agreed. Why argue? "I still think we need to talk with Al."

"You and me both. I'll meet you at his and Candy's house tomorrow morning. Surely he'll be back from wherever he went by then." She jotted down an address on a slip of paper and handed it to Jennifer.

"Okay, I guess I can manage that." She didn't need to have anything ready for Dee Dee until late Monday afternoon. "But I still think we have to focus on Danny. Do you remember anything different that happened, anything unusual, an out-of-the-ordinary reaction?"

Sheena paused for a moment and then stared at her. "Maybe. I've been working nonstop on the reunion for the past several months. I got a demo CD in the mail, from that guy Seth said something about Saturday night. I don't know what he expected me to do with it. Maybe play it that night if he didn't show up."

"You mean Gavin Lawless."

"Right. Lawless, Lawson, something like that. Danny walked in while I had it on. He asked me where I got it. Then he turned it off, took it out of the CD player, and put it in his pocket."

"Why?"

"I don't know. The song was a ballad about some kid everybody thought had run away. Sort of like what happened to—"

"Jimmy Mitchell," Jennifer finished.

Chapter 12

Some days refused to end, and it looked as though this was going to be one of them. At least Sheena was gone, and Jennifer had a chance to get out of her panty hose, into a shower, and then into clean shorts and a knit top.

Her headache was back, and so was the cold cloth, along with another dose of aspirin. She couldn't relax, no matter how deep she snuggled in the padding of her couch. She lay there, pretending to herself that she was resting, but actually listening with one ear for another assault on her door. In his note, Sam said he'd stop by later, and Teague McAfee had made her a promise.

McAfee was the kind of reporter that any scandal rag would love to have on staff. He was tenacious and unscrupulous. Indeed, to him, conscience was a mere theoretical concept. What made it worse, he was always hitting on her. He was five years her junior, clean-cut and as all-American looking as a four-letter athlete, only without the body. He tended to the skinny side. True, he had helped her once before, when Emma Walker was charged with murdering her ex-husband, but associating with Teague was like making a pact with the devil: whatever she might get out of it, he always expected a payback.

Sure enough, before another twenty minutes had passed, a knock sounded, setting Muffy off on an excited round of barking. When she reluctantly dragged herself up off the sofa to peer through the peephole, she saw Teague McAfee. He stood grinning back at her, one eyebrow raised as if he was sure she was looking at him.

"Go away. I'm not home," she told him.

"Sure you are. Your car's in the parking lot."

"I took a cab."

"Come on, Marsh, open up. It's your old friend Teague."

Maybe if she didn't make any more noise, he'd get frustrated and go away. She watched him purse his lips, grossly distorted through the warp of the peephole.

He took a notepad out of his pocket and seemed to be reading. "Former girlfriend Jennifer Marsh was extensively questioned by the police in the recent death of Daniel Buckner. Unable to reach her at home, this reporter spoke at some length with her neighbors who—"

Jennifer threw back the New York–style bar that she'd had installed after the break-in in her apartment several months ago and jerked open the door.

"How did you find out I dated Danny?" she demanded.

"So, these are your digs," he remarked, walking past her, totally ignoring what she'd said. He gave Muffy a good rub under her chin, and she danced in front of him.

"Bad dog!" Jennifer chastised, and Muffy slunk away.

Maybe if she simply reasoned with him . . . "No one in Atlanta is going to be interested in the death of anyone in Macon."

He turned and looked her in the face. "Of course they will. Some joker goes to his high school reunion and kills himself, maybe because of some unrequited, long-lost love." He winked at her. "It doesn't get any better than that. Besides, I got some great photos of the new widow defending her crown against a usurper. My readers will eat it up. Which reminds me, you hungry?"

If she'd disliked him before, she hated him now. "That joker—"

"Right. He was a friend of yours. My condolences." He whipped out the pad. "So why'd he kill himself?"

"Why are you here, Teague?"

"I couldn't endure another moment without the pleasure of your company."

"Right. But why, really?"

He shrugged. "I had an interview in town this morning. You know I couldn't come to Macon without stopping by."

"And why were you at the reunion last night?" She thought for a moment. "It's Ben Underwood, isn't it? You must have gotten a tip that he'd show up. You're not going to drag all that back up about Jimmy Mitchell's disappearance, are you? Can't you give the guy a break? He was only sixteen. . . ."

Teague was squinting at her with a little too much interest. The scoundrel was making mental notes. Drat! He must have gotten to the reunion after Underwood's little scene, and she'd be darned if she was going to tip Teague McAfee to a story.

"Did you say Ben or Len?" He scribbled something on the notepad.

She grabbed for it, but he jerked it back. "Uh-uh. That's a fourth- or fifth-degree assault, I forget which. Hands off, baby cakes. No one touches Teague's notes."

Just in case she didn't have enough reasons to despise Teague McAfee, she hated it when people referred to themselves in the third person.

"If it wasn't Underwood . . ."

"That's right. Gavin Lawless, up-and-coming music star. The next Bob Dylan."

"You would know this because . . ."

"Got a letter saying he was coming in for the reunion. With it was a promo CD with some very interesting lyrics."

"You, too?" Was she the only one south of the Mason-Dixon line who hadn't received one?

Teague looked around. He had that foraging look. His gaze lit on her energy stash sitting next to the computer. Helping himself, he peeled off the wrapper, popped the candy into his mouth, and savored the chocolate on his tongue. "The guy ain't half bad. Real smooth, kind of mellow."

"So you like his voice. Macon and Atlanta are full of musicians, good ones. If you wrote a story about every guitar player who came out of—"

"I didn't drive down here because the guy can sing."

She waited for him to go on. He chewed up the candy and swallowed, suddenly more serious than she'd ever seen him. "The song . . . it's . . . well, it's hard to describe. I guess you might say it's disturbing. The words . . . they seem to have an air of truth about them. Want to hear it?"

Oh yeah. It was high on her list of things to do after no sleep last night and an afternoon with Sheena and now Teague.

"How about later?" she suggested.

"After supper? Out? My treat."

"No supper," she assured him.

"Okay, now then." His gazed darted about the room before landing on the boom box on her desk.

Before she could protest, he pulled the disk out of his pocket, slipped it into the machine, and pressed Play.

Gavin's voice, low, full, and sincere, sang above the notes of a lone acoustic guitar.

"The rains came after midnight,
They washed the humid air,

Brought with them dreams of new day,
but he no longer cared.

Red clay was his companion,
Abandoned to the dust,
He'd sleep like that forever,
A victim of their trust.

The dawn broke cold on mornin',
They said he ran away,
Perhaps off west to Natchez,
But that's just what they say.

Someday I'll be back for ya,
Someday I will return,
Waiting's not forever,
Then it will be your turn.

Hey, hey, hey.
I'll be back for you.
On that you can rely,"

For just a moment, the music stopped and Gavin spoke the words:

"I promise."

Then he strummed the guitar and sang:

"I'll be back for you.
On that you can rely."

Jennifer stared at Teague, stunned. It was a threat. Plain and simple. Gavin Lawless had come back to Macon to seek revenge. But why? And against whom?

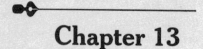

Chapter 13

Without a word, Jennifer went straight past Teague to the phone, punching in numbers as quickly as she could. Three rings. Would it be so difficult for Leigh Ann to simply pick up her phone?

The answering machine clicked on.

"Are you there, Leigh Ann? If you're screening your calls, I really, really need to talk to you," Jennifer sputtered into the receiver.

"You worried about your friend?" Teague asked.

"Why are you still here?"

For the first time since she'd met him, Teague seemed to have dropped the shield of arrogance he wrapped around himself. Then his eyes returned to normal, and Jennifer reminded herself not to be pulled into a false belief that he might actually be human.

She wasn't about to tell him anything, certainly not about Leigh Ann and her relation to one Gavin Lawless.

"The song got me rattled," she confessed, dropping the receiver into its cradle.

Teague nodded. "Why, I asked myself, would some dude write a song about a murder? I mean love seems to be the usual topic, don't you think?"

Not where Teague was concerned. Murder seemed far

more appropriate. "Did you come up with an answer?" she asked.

"Maybe. I looked at the guy's bio, the one he sent with the disk," he explained. "A native of Macon, twenty-eight years old, graduated ten years ago from his local high school, left home shortly thereafter, yadda yadda yadda. So I go back into the *Eye*'s archives, figuring this guy wants something from me, and I'm prepared to give it. Assuming I get something in return. I didn't find anything the last two years this dude was in Macon, but one more year back and voilà! One Jimmy Mitchell steps off the face of the earth, the night of the senior prom at Riverside High School, which just happens to be ol' Gavin's alma mater. Interesting coincidence considering the song lyrics, don't you think?"

Teague dropped his briefcase on her dining table and pulled out a stack of yellowing newsprint. Muffy snuffled at the corners, and paper dust puffed into the air.

Jennifer flipped through the stack, marveling at the creativity.

Macon Boy Abducted by Alien Ship. Area Boy Steps Through Time Warp. Disappearance Linked to Psycho Killer. Teenaged Maconite Suspected in Cult Disappearance.

"Are they all like this?" Jennifer asked, coming up for air. She flipped through the remaining stack.

Teague grinned at her. "No. I left the more outlandish ones back at the office."

"Could there be a kernel of truth buried deep down in one of these articles somewhere?"

"Not that I could tell. But you have to admire the journalist who can take a story with no facts, no witnesses, no body, and get a good month's worth of copy out of it."

No, she didn't.

"The paper protected the boy who was brought in for

questioning. Underwood? Was that his name? It never appeared in any of the articles."

She nodded.

"You say he's in town?"

She rolled her eyes at him.

"I did find something interesting." He tapped his pen on the newspapers. "Look on page two of the one on top."

"The abduction account?"

"Right."

She folded back the page. There it was, two paragraphs down. " 'Mitchell's aunt and uncle,' " Jennifer read aloud, " 'Mr. and Mrs. West Lawson, confirm that the family is putting together a reward for any information that leads to the discovery of the whereabouts of their nephew.' "

She let the paper slide back down onto the table and stared at Teague. "That means—"

"Right. Looks to me like Gavin Lawson and Jimmy Mitchell were first cousins."

"Family," Jennifer said to herself.

"Right. Family's supposed to look after family."

"What do you mean, look after?"

"Some people call it justice, Marsh. Other people call it murder. I call it a motive."

"What the heck are you talking about?" she demanded. "A motive for what?"

"Maybe nothing. Yet." He put the yellowed newsprint back in his briefcase, grabbed it up, and blew her a kiss as he moved toward the door. "Gotta go. Thanks for the tip about Underwood. Give me a call when you're ready to talk about Buckner. Remember, whatever you tell me—it doesn't have to be true."

"But—"

With that he closed the door in her face.

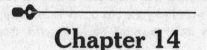

Chapter 14

It had to be there somewhere. Jennifer shoved a stack of manuscripts to one side on the top shelf of her closet and, standing on tiptoe, fished behind them. She knew she hadn't thrown it out. She couldn't have. It'd be like throwing out a piece of herself.

Her hand hit cardboard and closed around a flimsy shoe box that she dragged forward and then caught in both arms as it dove off the shelf. The contents rattled like old bones.

She carried it to the sofa and sat down on the floor Indian style, cradling the box. She hadn't looked inside in twelve years.

Opening it, she found the crushed corsage of red rosebuds, dried to a gray powder and nesting amidst lace, baby's breath, and faded white-satin ribbon. Gently, she set the corsage aside. Beneath it was her dance card from the prom. Danny had filled his name in on every line. She traced her hand over his illegible scrawl, the memory bringing an involuntary smile to her lips.

Farther down was her ticket stub from *Nightmare on Elm Street: the Dream Master,* the one and only film Danny had ever taken her to see. It had scared her so badly she'd practically climbed over the armrest at the theater and into his lap. Danny had loved every minute of it, and so had she.

Next were three snapshots her friend Megan had taken on

a senior class trip to Six Flags over Georgia. Danny made faces at the camera while hugging her to him on the back-seat of the bus. Her hair was flat, soaked from the water rides, but her whole face was a grin, hiding her embarrassment. They were lucky the bus driver hadn't stopped and put the noisy lot of them off. She'd forgotten that they'd ever gone.

They all looked so *young*. Not that she was old, she reminded herself.

Beneath the photos, she found the corner she'd torn off Danny's science notebook when he playfully hit her over the head with it; the straw he'd presented to her in the cafeteria, jokingly, as a token of his affection; and the hot-pink slap bracelet he'd clamped onto her wrist before school one morning. She touched each item and then set it aside, as if too much handling might somehow erase the memories.

Tucked in one corner was a folded piece of pink paper. She pulled it out and opened it. *Don't date him. You'll be sorry if you do,* she read. Oh, yes. Now she remembered. Sheena's fond farewell. She'd found it, unsigned, slipped through the vent in her locker. One more example of Sheena's unrelenting persecution. Why had she kept it? She studied the round, bubble letters with the circles dotting the *i*s and then it came back to her. The note had come the week after prom night, after her breakup with Danny. She'd kept it as a handwriting sample to take with her to the office if Sheena did one more hateful thing to her. It was the first and only hard evidence that Sheena had given to her of all the hateful things she'd done. But the harassment had stopped, and the note served as one final reminder of all the agony Sheena put her through. She tossed it aside.

In the bottom of the box lay her journal, shining beneath everything else. The cover was one of those silver, optical patterns that danced in the light, the sort of ultratacky, all-that-glitters design that only teenage girls buy.

She'd hoped she still had it, that it was in the box with the rest. She pulled it out, her heart beating a little too fast. Did she really want to hear her own words, experience those emotions again?

She flipped it open and leafed through it. Danny's name was everywhere. The early entries had been written before the two of them were actually talking, when he was still throwing looks at her across the hallway and pretending to walk into walls when he saw her.

Sheena's name was just as prominent. If hatred had a persona, it used too much makeup and bleached its hair brittle.

Several pages over, Jennifer and Danny's relationship had progressed.

Tuesday. Danny asked me out again. I lied and told him I didn't like him, but I really do. Sheena is sooooo angry. She and her friends glare at me in the hall and whisper when I walk by. I got another one of those weird phone messages last night. This one was from an Air Force recruiter saying he'd gotten my application. I wonder if Danny knows what she's been doing.

Wednesday. Two guys I don't know stopped me in the hall and asked me what kind of "services" I provide. I asked Joey what was going on. He told me not to worry about it. He'd scrubbed my name off of the wall in the boys' bathroom. I HATE her!!!!!

Thursday. He is soooooo cute. He waited for me after math class today. He had two tuna fish sandwiches (really gross), a big bag of chips, and two Cokes. We found a place behind the gym to eat lunch, somewhere

Sheena couldn't find us. The tuna fish was yucky, but I ate it anyway. I told him I'd go out with him.

Jennifer skipped through pages. She didn't need to live through every minute of swooning over Danny or playing hide and seek with Sheena. She'd been so naive, her own words made her cringe.

Friday. Danny didn't call me tonight. Sometimes I think I actually hate him. He's the most inconsiderate jerk I've ever known. I just hope nothing's wrong.

Monday. Danny seemed upset at school today. He wouldn't tell me why, but he apologized for not calling. I think Sheena's bothering him, too. Or maybe it's that crowd of his. I don't know why he hangs out with them. Al is so stuck-up, Mick is gorgeous but truly weird, and Seth doesn't care about anybody but himself. He did wink at me and say hi in the hall today, though. He had some new girl on his arm as usual.

Tuesday. Lunch again with Danny. He seemed distracted, but he wouldn't tell me why.

Wednesday. Danny is soooo moody. I'm almost sorry I agreed to go to the prom with him. I found the most gorgeous dress ever at Macy's. I can't believe Mom actually bought it for me.

Friday. Tonight's the prom. I'm sooooooo excited. I'm writing this while my nails dry. That's why the letters are all squiggly. It will be perfect. I know it will.

Several of the pages following the last note were torn out. She ran her fingers over the jagged edge. She had written about that night in detail, then yanked out the entries and burned them. They'd been too painful to keep. Drat it all. If anything of importance was in that journal, it would have been on those pages.

Two pages over she found a final entry.

Seth Yarborough actually asked me out.

She paused. She'd forgotten. Then she read on.

I told him no. I'm never going to date anybody ever again.

Jennifer closed the journal of her young self's dreams, leaned back against the sofa, and let the tears welling in her eyes spill. There was a part of her that would forever care for eighteen-year-old Danny Buckner.

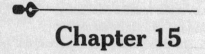

Chapter 15

She was actually meeting Sheena Buckner, like more-or-less civilized adults. Why, of all the people in Macon, did they have to be the only two who believed Danny Buckner was murdered?

Jennifer's little Volkswagen Beetle putted up to the curb in front of the circular driveway of a huge Victorian mansion located not far from downtown on College Street. She rolled down the window, letting in the pleasant morning air, and checked the address Sheena had given her for Al Carpenter's house, scribbled on a piece of paper. The numbers on the plaque sticking out of the grass at the edge of the street matched. She wondered briefly if Sheena could have copied it down wrong.

Then she spied Sheena waiting for her in a red Jeep Cherokee parked directly in front of the door in the circular driveway. This was the place all right.

Jennifer backed up, getting closer to the curb, pulled on the emergency brake, cut the engine, and opened the car door.

Sheena, her hair pulled back in a ponytail, and dressed in white shorts that showed off her tanned, muscular legs and a red halter top that showed off her other attributes, was at her door and hurrying her up. Interesting attire for a new widow.

"What the heck are you driving?" Sheena asked, giving

the Beetle a good once-over. "God, Jenny. Can't you even afford a car? All you need is a big daisy painted on the side and you'd look like you stepped out of the Sixties."

"It's a classic," Jennifer insisted defensively. She didn't bother to add that it had indeed once had a daisy painted on its side, shortly after her mom first bought it. "I'm restoring it." One piece at a time, as each piece wore out.

She wasn't about to get drawn into a discussion on economics. Have-it-all-have-it-now Sheena couldn't possibly understand the investment she was making with her writing, that careers in the arts took time to build. Besides, what was the use? The woman simply wouldn't be interested.

Jennifer peered at Sheena. She looked as though she hadn't slept since the last time they'd talked. Those little telltale lines around her eyes were getting deeper.

"I'm surprised you have time to come over here," Jennifer said. "I thought you might have things you had to do. Maybe make financial arrangements . . ."

"Nothing that can't wait. Danny left me insurance, lots of insurance, so don't you waste your time worrying about my finances," Sheena explained, as though talking to a three-year-old.

As if she would. Concern was lost on the Sheena Cassidys of this world. She was her own tower of strength, one whose foundations, Jennifer suspected, stood on shifting sands.

"I called Candy," Sheena explained as they walked to the door. "She still hasn't heard from Al, unless he dragged his sorry carcass home in the twenty minutes it took me to drive over here."

"So why are we—"

"You give me someplace else to start and we'll be there." Sheena leaned on the doorbell.

A vaguely familiar, short, round woman with shiny, bright

red hair opened the door. She was dressed in a flowing green-print caftan, and she was cute, really cute, with a cheery, dimpled smile that would have made Jennifer grin back under different circumstances. She was also heavy enough that a vision of her doing splits at the top of a pyramid made Jennifer understand why she'd skipped the reunion. Too bad. She had a feeling she probably would like this version of Candy better than the perfect model of popularity she'd most likely been sixty pounds ago.

Candy hugged Sheena and then stepped back, her face gone slack, and shook her head as though fighting for words. She managed to croak out, "You doin' all right, hon?"

"That husband of yours back yet?" Sheena demanded, ever charming.

"You know Al as well as I do. He'll be back when he gets back." Candy looked at Jennifer, a puzzled expression on her face. "You didn't mention . . ."

"Jennifer Marsh," she said, offering the woman her hand.

Candy drew back, her gaze darting back and forth between Sheena and Jennifer before landing with a piercing stare on Jennifer's face. "Not *the* Jennifer . . ."

"Yes, *the* Jennifer that stole Danny away from Sheena in high school." She smiled and raised one eyebrow at the scowl on Sheena's face. "Don't be so touchy. I gave him back."

"*Gave* him back," Sheena roared.

"Ladies, please," Candy insisted, stepping between the two women. She turned her back on Sheena and ushered Jennifer inside, whispering, "You know, I thought you looked familiar." Then she turned back to her friend and offered a few words under her breath that Jennifer couldn't quite make out. She did catch "not here" and "You know how Danny felt about you."

Sheena threw Jennifer a glare and pushed past her into the large, tiled foyer.

"I made coffee," Candy offered, "and there are doughnuts in the fridge if anybody wants some."

She led them to the back of the house and a bright, airy, all-white kitchen with glass doors that opened onto a high deck decorated with hanging baskets of bright pink impatiens. Then she busied herself near the sink.

"I want to know why Al has been hounding Danny to meet with him for the past week when none of us have seen each other in years," Sheena said.

Candy turned back around, coffee carafe in hand. "Sheena, you should know that Al never tells me anything, but I'm sure it must be because of the reunion." She pulled two large mugs from a stand and filled them with coffee. Then she shooed the women to the wooden table, setting a mug in front of each of them, and took her own seat, sans coffee, next to Sheena.

"Al does his thing, I do mine. It makes for a perfect marriage." She pushed the cream and sugar toward Jennifer, along with a spoon and napkin that were already on the table.

"You don't worry when he goes off like this?" Jennifer couldn't keep herself from asking. Why marry if two people were only going to share real estate? And genetic material. She'd noticed a child's bike leaned up against the house, so the Carpenters had at least one offspring.

"When Al gets going on a case, he can work around the clock. He's probably at the office."

"He's not," Sheena told her. "I called."

For some inexplicable reason, Jennifer felt convinced, Candy had called Al's office, too.

"At a hotel, then," Candy offered, her hands shaking ever

so slightly. She seemed practiced at making excuses for Al. "He has trouble working at home. The kids are noisy."

Something wasn't right here. Candy was nervous, and she was as unhelpful as her manners would allow her to be.

"What kind of practice does Al have?" Jennifer asked.

"Criminal law, mostly."

"Who does he use as private investigators?" Jennifer fished.

"There's a firm on the other side of town. He likes it because they have a female operative in addition to the three men. He says women can sometimes get information when men can't. Why do you ask?"

"Just curious." She didn't point out that Danny hadn't called Al Carpenter when he'd needed a detective. "You see, I write mystery novels."

Candy brightened. "You do? Can I buy one?"

She knew not to mention it. . . .

"A week or so ago, Danny started acting funny," Sheena broke in, as though she hadn't heard what they'd said. "I thought I overheard him talking to Al on the phone. Did Danny call here?"

"Why, yes," Candy assured her. "I answered the phone when Danny called."

"Could you tell what they were talking about?" Jennifer asked.

"I didn't even bother. I figured it was just two old friends catching up."

"The phone calls from Al started coming after that," Sheena told them.

"Why are you two asking all these questions?" Candy asked. "I expected you to have your hands full with . . . well, with the arrangements for Danny."

The doorbell bonged three notes, like a Chinese gong.

"If you'll excuse me . . ." Candy got up, again glancing

between Sheena and Jennifer, this time as though she were afraid to leave them alone, afraid of what they might do to one another. Then she disappeared down the hall.

"This is a waste of time," Sheena announced. "Al has that woman so cowed she'll do anything, say anything, he wants her to."

"Maybe she simply doesn't know anything," Jennifer pointed out. "Or maybe she's just loyal. He *is* her husband. What was that you said earlier about not seeing each other in years?"

"Danny and I never socialized with Al and Candy, not since high school."

"But I thought the four of you were tight."

"Danny and Al's group fell apart after the prom."

"Why?" Jennifer asked.

Sheena shrugged. "I was busy getting back together with Danny after he dumped you."

"He did not dump me," Jennifer insisted, amazed she still cared that that particular part of her history be recorded correctly. "I'm the one—"

Shouting echoed down the hall, freezing them in place, but only for a few seconds. Jennifer leaped out of her chair, with Sheena right behind her.

At the front door Candy stood red-faced, veins popping out on the sides of her neck. "He's not here, I told you. You can tell Seth Yarborough I don't care how many clerks he sends over here *as a personal favor*. I'm not my husband's keeper."

The young man, much taller and thinner than Candy, shrank back. "Ma'am, we're only trying to help. When the court appoints an attorney, he must show up for trial. If Mr. Carpenter isn't down at the courthouse within thirty minutes, he could be held in contempt of court. Maybe even arrested."

"Good. You find him. You arrest him. Now get out and leave me alone."

"Is there anything we can do to help?" Jennifer asked.

"Go," Candy roared again, but this time at Sheena and Jennifer.

She pushed the lot of them out the door and slammed it behind them, leaving Jennifer and Sheena facing a very bewildered young law clerk who immediately turned and walked away.

Chapter 16

"I can see why Danny was so drawn to you," Seth told Jennifer, wiping his mouth with his lunch napkin and letting it play peekaboo with his smile.

She offered her best pleased-as-punch, hopefully not-too-artificial grin. He could be "drawn" to her, too, as long as Yarborough didn't suspect why she was drawn to him. She'd love to know why he felt it necessary to send a law clerk to fetch Carpenter to court that morning—on a case Yarborough wasn't even involved with. She'd called and checked the morning's docket and spoken with a very helpful clerk. Could just be that Seth was simply helping a friend. Wasn't that the way it was supposed to be?

Or it could be that he suspected Al of something.

"I'm glad you let me talk you into having lunch," he added.

She studied him. He was all charm. Too bad she couldn't relax and enjoy it without trying to read some deep motive into everything he said. Of course, the fact that she still hadn't been able to reach Leigh Ann by phone, and nobody answered the knock on the door when she dropped by her apartment on the way over to Applebee's, wasn't helping her nerves, either. Leigh Ann's car was in her apartment building parking lot, and all her boss had heard was a terse request for sick leave left on her voice mail sometime late

Sunday night. Please Lord, just let her be all right and anywhere other than with Gavin Lawless.

Now, she tried to concentrate on Seth Yarborough's
chatter. He had never said much more than two words to her
in high school—although her journal did attest he asked her
out once—so why, she wondered, had he suddenly taken
such an interest in her? Did he think they'd bonded over
Danny's death? One little hug did not a bond make.

"I was surprised to get your call this morning. I wouldn't
think you'd have time for lunch," she said. "Aren't you usually in court?"

"Not today."

"Ever go up against Al Carpenter?" She speared an elusive piece of romaine from her Caesar salad and held it
poised at her lips.

"On occasion."

"Is he any good?"

"You should have ordered the fried chicken salad," he
told her, savoring a bite.

She didn't care to get into the whole vegetarian debate,
especially when he was already doing a good job of dis-
tracting her.

"I went over the statement you gave to the police," he
told her.

Oh. So this wasn't a personal lunch. It was business.
Assistant district attorney business. And the smiles and the
charm, maybe that was business, too.

"It was short and to the point," he went on, scraping out
the last bit of honey-mustard dressing from a round, porce-
lain container.

"I didn't have more than a minute or two with Danny
before Al Carpenter showed up and whisked him away.
Like he did . . ." She paused when she realized her mouth
was running away with her thoughts.

"Like he did what?"

"Nothing. Danny didn't tell me anything. Apparently he wanted me to suggest the name of a private investigator."

That made Seth frown. "Why?"

"I wouldn't know. Like I said, we were interrupted."

"So you don't have any idea why he would kill himself."

"None at all. Before the reunion, I hadn't talked to him since high school."

Why did people think she would know something? Sheena and now Seth. It would help if they'd let her in on what it was.

"You were his friend," Jennifer pointed out.

"That was a long time ago."

Jennifer nodded. It seemed like another lifetime. "What happened? Why did your foursome break up?"

"You'd have to ask Al about that. He and Danny had some kind of falling out."

"Prom night?" she suggested.

"Around then. Look, Jennifer, don't get trapped in the past. Danny killed himself now, and now is when we're going to find the answers. How did you find his mood? Did he seemed depressed?"

All these questions seemed strange coming from someone she'd seen in Danny's company, but she knew an investigator was always reluctant to serve as a witness.

"No," she said. "Maybe a little anxious."

"That wouldn't be unusual for someone about to take his own life."

"How'd he seem to you?" she asked.

Seth smiled and refilled her wineglass.

He'd answered one personal question. She had a feeling she wouldn't get another.

"You know," he said, "when we were kids, I always expected you and Danny would someday get married."

That comment stopped her fork full of salad in mid sweep. She blushed deeply. *She'd* never thought it. "Why?"

He shrugged, that smile still in place. "I don't know. It just seemed that there was something special between the two of you, that you could talk to each other, confide in each other, share secrets. His marriage to Sheena . . . well, that came as a surprise."

"They dated for years," Jennifer reminded him, and then let the fork complete its journey.

"Yeah, and that surprised me, too. She can be a bit of a shrew when she's crossed."

And when she's not. But someplace deep down in her repressed memories, Jennifer was digging up a nugget. "Didn't you date her? Maybe the beginning of our junior year?"

"I wouldn't have called it dating. We went out twice, I think it was."

"If I remember correctly, she obsessed about you—"

"For another two months. Until I set her straight. She latched onto Danny shortly after that."

"How lucky for you."

He smiled. "And unlucky for you. Did you ever get the bubble gum out of your locker?"

So he remembered, too. "Nope. Got fined for that one."

"How many pieces did she use?"

"Hard to tell. At least two packs." It seemed funny now, but then . . . "Sheena thinks Danny was murdered," she said, watching for his reaction.

"Yes, I'm well aware of Sheena's suspicions." He took a sip of wine.

"You don't seem concerned."

"It's not unusual for a spouse to go into denial, especially about a suicide. We'll keep an open mind throughout the investigation, of course, but at the moment it looks as though Danny killed himself."

She nodded. What was she supposed to do? Tell him how to do his job?

"You said Danny sent you a note?" he added.

"Right. In the mail, asking me to come to the reunion."

"I'd like to see it."

"I don't have it with me."

"Fine. Send it to me at the office. I want to close out this case, so we can release the body and let Sheena bury her husband."

"But why do you need—"

"We're trying to establish Danny's state of mind. Since we didn't find a suicide note, we have to reconstruct the last days and weeks of his life by interviewing everyone he had contact with. It's just routine. He was obviously despondent over something."

Despondent over something. The words echoed in her ears. If so, he certainly hid it well.

"He'd made an appointment with an attorney for some-time this week," Seth said.

"Why?" she asked.

"I wouldn't want to speculate."

"What kind of attorney?"

"Family law."

"You can't mean to tell me—"

"Whatever problems Danny may have had with Sheena, I'm sure he planned to work them out."

"Are you saying Danny was considering divorce?"

Seth shook his head. "Of course not. Danny didn't tell his attorney what it was he wished to speak with him about. It's probably best that way. Suicide leaves plenty of guilt to go around as it is."

He glanced at his watch and downed the rest of his wine.

"Sorry to have to run off. Maybe we can do this again. Soon, I hope."

"Perhaps."

"Don't forget to send me the note. Right away."

She nodded, a little stunned. Maybe Sheena was insisting that Danny was murdered only because she couldn't face his suicide. Still, in her own gut, she felt certain Danny had been murdered. If she'd had anything at all to offer Seth, she would have gladly shared it, but intuition wasn't worth spit in a court of law.

So how, exactly, was she going to get proof that someone murdered Danny when the assistant district attorney didn't believe it?

Chapter 17

Intellectually, Jennifer knew that Sheena's personality in and of itself made a good case for Danny's death being a suicide. If she had to live with that woman, she would have slit her wrists ages ago. But even if Seth seemed convinced, he'd failed to sway her. In her bones she knew it was murder. Somehow. Some way.

One more time, Jennifer checked the return address on the envelope Danny had sent her, and studied the house from the shelter of her Volkswagen Beetle parked across the narrow street. The heat from the afternoon sun was broken by the tall trees that shaded the road.

The generous lot allowed for a large, manicured front lawn that sloped gently and then rose back up to meet the road. The house itself, a lots-of-glass contemporary design, sat far enough back amidst azaleas and rhododendrons to be quite striking in the shadows of the tall pine trees. It looked brand-new. Couldn't be more than a couple of years old. She suspected it was custom built. She noticed that it had a two-car garage.

She wondered what it must be like to live there. With Danny. Or with anybody else. Mowing grass, cooking meals— real meals, not microwave miracles. Washing windows, lots and lots of windows. Entertaining on the deck out back.

(She couldn't see it, but she felt sure there had to be one. Maybe even a pool.)

Had they been happy? Danny and Sheena?

Is this what she wanted? Jennifer wondered. Had she ever wanted it? Is this what their life would have been if she and Danny . . .

She shook her head. Something would always be missing. She probably never would have found the courage to write, maybe never even realized she wanted to. If she had, would Danny have understood?

Why was she wasting her time speculating about life with a dead man whom, if she were honest with herself, she had never really known?

Because she'd seen a spark in Danny, some kind of goodness or humanity that drew her to him. It couldn't have all been hormones.

And because he was dead, and he shouldn't be.

And because Seth Yarborough had raised the question in her mind.

She pulled out the yellow pad that had fallen between the seats and studied her notes. After coming back from Candy's and before going to lunch with Yarborough, she'd spent the morning with the phone sandwiched between her ear and her shoulder while she mixed dill weed dip for Dee Dee. She'd long since discovered that getting information was easy. Making sense out of what she found out was a whole other matter. Keeping artichoke salad off the receiver was even harder.

Mick Farmer and Danny had been as tight as any two friends, tight enough to venture into business together. If Danny didn't confide in Sheena, the next most likely person would be Mick.

She let her pen circle Macon Pictures and rolled her eyes. It seemed Danny and Mick weren't above using a corny pun. They were everywhere in the city. At least it wasn't as obvious as the hockey team, the Macon Whoopees.

A lovely sounding woman had answered the phone that morning and was more than happy to help with her inquiries. Yes, they were a video postproduction company. If she brought them her raw footage, they could edit it, put in, adjust, or alter the sound, and add titles, credits, headings, or subtitles. They could also brighten or darken, at least to some degree, and suggest additional scenes or shots as needed. They'd been established for six years, and she could assure her that even with the death of Mr. Buckner, business would continue as usual. Mr. Farmer would see to that.

Mr. Farmer. Mr. Michael Farmer. Mick.

He and Danny must have complemented one another well. Mick was the artistic one, Danny the practical one.

And now Mick was the sole proprietor. Not Mick and Sheena. Just Mick, whose idea had created the business in the first place. Sounded like a survivorship clause. And a possible motive. If Danny was indeed murdered. Plus a bonus: Sheena would be free to remarry.

Some bonus.

But some fantasies are hard to let go of. Ask Jay Gatsby.

Mick, with his dark, hunky good looks. Mick who had never married. Mick, who, being the artist he was, could appreciate suffering, which would stand him in good stead if he ever did hook up with Sheena.

Jennifer cranked the engine and reached in the back to make sure the four large containers filled with canapés and the two small ones with the dip and salad were secure on the seat before she took off. She had to get them to Dee Dee's before three for a drop-off at four.

The Buckners' home wasn't too far out of the way. Her little Bug had practically found its way there on its own.

So now she'd seen it. It was time to go. She had her own life to lead, and she'd do well to remember it. If she hurried, she might even be able to get home in time to write a few pages before she went to her writers' meeting that night. She hadn't shown the group anything for two weeks. She'd never get a novel finished at that rate.

The notepad slipped off her lap and dropped again between the front seats as she took one final glance at Danny's home.

"I'll do what I can to find out what happened to you, Danny," she whispered. "I'm so sorry you had to die." She was well aware of how ridiculously overdramatic she must seem. But there was no one to listen, no one to judge, no one to ridicule, and she meant it. She would.

She knew exactly where to begin. She needed to get inside Macon Pictures without arousing Mick Farmer's suspicions. Mick wasn't one to be bullied or to volunteer information openly, if he was anything like he'd been in high school. He rarely, if ever, had confided in anyone that she knew of. So if she wanted any information, she'd have to take a subtle approach, and she knew exactly who could help her get inside the business.

Teri had been caught by the acting bug in high school. She'd even tried her hand at the community theater, but that hadn't gone too well. Teri wasn't one to take direction or to deliver lines verbatim. She had a problem with embellishment. The gift of imagination that fueled her stories did some real damage to her ability to memorize.

Nevertheless, she did own a video camera, and she had known enough to catch their writers' group on tape one time when they'd all gone to the beach. Maybe she needed a little advice with a project. Maybe she needed to speak with Mick Farmer about what he could do for her once she'd finished shooting whatever it was she might possibly be shooting. Jennifer would have called Teri and set up an appointment, but not today. They had group tonight, and it was best not to bring it up then. She knew her fellow writers all too well. They'd have a full-length feature film plotted with a part written for each of them before their meeting was over. Yes, it was a great idea, and one that would get her closer to one Mick Farmer, a friend from Danny's past and a business partner from his present. A man who just might have some answers.

Finally, she pushed the gear lever into drive and just then caught a flicker of motion in her peripheral vision.

The front door opened and Sheena came outside, broom in hand. Quickly, she swept the small front porch and then the sidewalk, beating the pavement with sufficient force to bend the broom straw. She hadn't quite reached the driveway when she abandoned the broom against the house and dropped to her knees, frantically tearing at something in the flower bed between the walk and the front of the house. Must be weeds, Jennifer thought. Sheena tossed something green over her shoulder, apparently not caring if it found root elsewhere. Then she grabbed up the broom once more and attacked the cement drive. Halfway down she stopped abruptly, letting the broom fall to the pavement. She covered her face with both hands and sank to her knees.

Feeling a pity she knew Sheena would detest, Jennifer pulled out into the road and drove away.

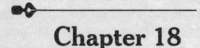

Chapter 18

Writing. It was Jennifer's anchor, her link to sanity if not to reality, the one thing that kept her focused in an otherwise chaotic universe. Not that her Monday night writers' group couldn't be chaotic. Or unfocused. Or . . .

"Go ahead, Teri," Monique commanded, firmly rooted in her rocking chair, her leadership of this small band of young would-be writers unquestionable.

Teri, who was lying on her stomach and propped up on her elbows in front of Monique's sectional sofa, had been periodically touching the back of her head with her bare feet. The woman was a human pretzel, a fact that irked Jennifer as only genetic abilities could.

Teri straightened out, swung her legs around, and dug in her briefcase for the pages from her latest romantic suspense novel.

Jennifer, sitting next to Teri on the floor, her own legs stretched out and ankles crossed, reminded herself that she had to keep her mind on tonight's readings. She owed at least that much to this group who tried so hard to help her get published, but thoughts of Sheena kept tugging at her.

Their stroll down memory lane yesterday afternoon had emphasized only that Jennifer and Sheena had lived in very different worlds back then—Sheena working the popular crowd, Jennifer hanging more quietly with her friends.

They'd known different people and frequented different hangouts. Their two worlds would probably never have overlapped if it hadn't been for Danny Buckner. And now they'd overlapped again.

While going through the past was fine, it ignored one important fact: for some reason, Gavin Lawless's song about Jimmy Mitchell's disappearance had upset Danny.

April let out an unintentionally loud yawn and then excused herself in a strained, high-pitched voice as she unsuccessfully tried to stifle it. She sat on the opposite couch, quietly munching raisins. She no longer had time to bake the goodies she was so fond of bringing to these meetings. Which was just as well since she had made it known how much she resented the extra ten pounds that refused to go away and let her get back to her pre-pregnancy weight.

Her pleasantly round face was marred by dark circles, and her blond hair, usually loosely waved, looked as if it hadn't met up with a curling iron in months. She seemed tired to the bone, and well she should. The delightful bundle making sweet little sleeping baby sounds in the carrier at her feet had been keeping her up every night for the last eight months. Add three-year-old Jonathan running day duty, and sleep had become a fond memory and a mere hope for the future. She hadn't produced more than a handful of pages for her children's stories since little Colette's birth, even though one publisher had expressed serious interest in the series. Yet April seemed happy, deep-down happy if not bubbly-surface happy. Jennifer could tell.

Sheena and Danny never had children. Their decision or God's?

She glanced behind her at the vacant spot on the sofa that Leigh Ann usually occupied. She never missed group, so where the heck was she? Group was Leigh Ann's last chance. If she didn't show tonight, Jennifer was filing a missing person's report.

Worrying about Leigh Ann had become one more nagging nuisance in an already difficult last three days. If Danny was murdered, the murderer had to have been at the reunion, or at the very least, on the school grounds that night, the night when Leigh Ann was last seen with one Gavin Lawless. The Gavin Lawless who had no more sense than to make a blatant threat in a song he distributed over most of Georgia. So who exactly was Gavin threatening? Only one person had died. It couldn't have been Danny. He would never have harmed anyone, let alone someone like Jimmy.

Teri cleared her throat, holding up some printed pages. "This is a continuation of *Desperate Passions*, the one where he's a biotechnical engineer and she's the cub reporter trying to expose him as a secret agent. The last chapter ended with Wilbur Burroughs coming home earlier than expected while Chandra was going through his personal items to look for the stolen DNA analysis. This opens right after she's slipped into his closet to hide."

"Wait up," April interrupted. "Isn't Wilbur your hero, the one Chandra is supposed to fall in love with?"

Teri nodded.

"I don't like his name," April insisted. "I told you before I thought you should change it. Burroughs is fine, but Wilbur—"

"I agree," Monique stated emphatically. "It raises the image of Mr. Ed."

"Mr. Ed?" Teri asked.

"The talking horse. Wilbur was the guy who talked to the horse."

"Who remembers a—"

"Still plays on cable, so don't tell me I'm old and out of

touch." It was a challenge, not one that any of them was likely to take up. Monique was somewhere in her forties, and woe to the person who pointed it out. Besides, it was her house.

"Don't forget the pig in *Charlotte's Web*," April added. "His name was Wilbur, too."

"My point exactly. Too many animal references. If you feel compelled to stay with a similar sounding name," Monique instructed, "I'd suggest Will or William, which has gained even greater respect of late with the overwhelming popularity of the young prince—"

"Right. Will Smith," Teri agreed.

Monique glared at her. "I was referring to the heir to the British throne, not the Fresh Prince of Bel Air. Actually, even better than William is its nickname Liam. It's in vogue right now. Remember, popular actor names are almost always a sure bet."

"I happen to like—" Teri began.

"Character names," Monique continued, warming to her lecture opportunity, "must be selected with regard to the type of role they'll play in the book. A hero must have a heroic name. Unfortunately, Wilbur, a perfectly good name, has been opted for some not-so-romantic uses. I suppose it could be a villain's name or the name of a minor character, but in this context it simply won't do. Maybe before the horse—"

"And the pig," April chimed in.

"—but not now," Monique continued. "I'd hate to see your work rejected for so simple an error. Remember, we're fighting unconscious associations every time an editor or an agent reads our work. Do you really think *Gone with the Wind* would have been a runaway bestseller if Margaret Mitchell hadn't changed her heroine's name from Pansy to Scarlett?"

"All right. Point taken." Teri rolled her eyes. "So do you or don't you want me to read tonight?"

"Read," Monique instructed her.

" 'Chandra held her breath as Wilbur—' "

April shuddered. "See what I mean? Chandra and Wilbur? They're phonetically incompatible."

"Okay, okay." Teri was no longer amused. "I'll change it."

Monique raised an eyebrow at April, her indication that no more interruptions would be tolerated.

" 'Chandra held her breath as Wilbur moved about the room. She could barely see his expensive Italian shoes through the downward slats of the closet door, but the unmistakable scent of his imported aftershave wafted into the enclosed space and made her head reel, reminding her of their last encounter at the dock when he'd pulled her from the choppy waters and held her in his arms, his thick biceps engulfing her with his strength. Her head had nestled against his neck, and his deep Barry White voice resonated from the sleek coppery skin of his sinewy throat.

" 'She wanted to trust him, almost as much as she wanted him, but did she dare? Two people were already dead and Wilbur had been the first on the scene of every homicide. He was either one step ahead of the police, one step behind the murderer, or . . . She couldn't bring herself to even think it. If she wasn't careful, trusting him could make her the next victim of the deadly Passion Bay murderer.' "

Too bad Leigh Ann wasn't there to hear that last sentence, Jennifer mused. Wilbur was a hero—they'd all read Teri's synopsis—but it was too soon to know which side, friend or foe, Gavin Lawless would fall on.

Just as Teri turned the page and drew in a great breath of air, they heard the front door swing open. Leigh Ann rushed in with a flustered, "I'm here, I'm here. What did I miss?"

She plopped onto the sectional. Her face was flushed, her hair in disarray.

Thank God she was all right. Actually better than all right. Leigh Ann looked prettier than Jennifer had ever seen her.

"Shhh," Monique warned.

Leigh Ann covered her mouth, whispered, "I'm sorry," kicked off her shoes, and curled her feet up on the sofa cushion.

Jennifer grabbed her hand and asked, "Where the heck have you been?"

Leigh Ann drew in a great gulp of air, but Teri swatted at them with her pages. Jennifer dropped Leigh Ann's hand and turned around like a good little critique partner. They would talk later.

"So glad you could join us," Teri said, too sweetly to be sincere. "You need to get your phone fixed, my friend. It obviously won't allow you to make outgoing calls."

Teri had been worried, too.

"I'll let you take home the part you missed," she told Leigh Ann, and then began reading again.

" 'Wilbur slipped off his loafers. She could only see the lower half of him through the slits. He pulled open a dresser drawer and drew out a pair of navy-blue silk pajamas. If he put them on and slipped into bed, Chandra could be stuck in that closet all night. She squirmed . . .' "

Jennifer would like to stick Leigh Ann in a closet. Better there than who knew where with Gavin, doing who knew what.

At least Leigh Ann was accounted for. That left Al Carpenter, and where he was was anybody's guess. Sheena said she'd last seen him shortly after she collapsed in his arms and right before the police arrived. Al had been one of the first on the scene, and the one who called 911. He told Sheena he needed to take care of something, but that had been two days ago. He still hadn't made it in to work as of six o'clock this evening. She'd checked before coming to Monique's. But he'd have to show up eventually. Or, at the very least, telephone his wife, Candy.

She wanted to talk to Sam. He had never made it over to her apartment Sunday. He'd called late, waking her up, to say a body had been found in an abandoned house along Route 74 about one o'clock that afternoon. He promised to see her later that night. She remembered thinking that it'd be good to see him, to have some time alone together. She'd been horrid to him at the reunion. Maybe she could make it up to him, and maybe he could help take her mind off Danny's death.

" 'Wilbur's full lips found her own and . . .' "

Jennifer smiled. Romantic suspense. She couldn't help but love it. Her mind strayed for no more than thirty seconds and ol' Chandra had made it out of that closet and into Wilbur's waiting arms. No wonder readers adored the genre. The reader could always be sure, despite how he was portrayed, the man the heroine fell in love with was a good guy. Too bad that wasn't true in real life.

Leigh Ann nudged her shoulder and leaned down. "Want to grab a bite later?" she whispered.

Monique glared at them, and for a moment Jennifer was afraid that Monique was going to ask them to share with everyone what Leigh Ann had said, and they'd all wind up having "a bite." Like having to distribute bubble gum to an entire class for getting caught chewing it. It wasn't easy trying to divide two sticks of gum into thirty-three pieces.

Jennifer nodded. She wasn't about to let Leigh Ann get away from her now. She tossed Monique a challenging look.

" '. . . and Chandra and Wilbur sank back against the soft satin of his sheets.' " Teri laid the papers in her lap.

"Comments?" Monique asked.

"Seems to me Chandra isn't thinking with her head," April observed. "Sex is fine in its place, but when you let it interfere with your reasoning powers, well, it just makes us women look foolish. She can't sleep with some guy she thinks may be a murderer. Come on!"

"I agree," Jennifer said, turning to look directly at Leigh Ann. "It's ridiculous. A woman should never fool around with a man she barely knows. Right, Leigh Ann?"

"Right," Leigh Ann repeated, smiling as though she'd missed Jennifer's point entirely.

Jennifer sighed. What really mattered, she supposed, was that Leigh Ann was safe. Even if only for the moment.

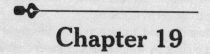

Chapter 19

"I'm in love," Leigh Ann declared, chomping on an over-filled eclair while sitting in a slick, molded plastic booth at the all-night bakery around the corner from Monique's house. Her tongue fished for and found the bit of vanilla cream filling caught in the corner of her mouth.

Leigh Ann had used the L word. This could not be good, not good at all.

"You can't be," Jennifer blurted out, suddenly not at all interested in her bear claw. It had looked so good not two seconds before. "I mean you've only spent how long with this guy?"

"Actually one evening, two fun-filled days, and two glorious nights." She sounded like she was describing a give-away vacation on some game show. "Besides, I've known him for years."

Leigh Ann took another huge bite. Apparently love had done great things for her appetite.

"That doesn't count," Jennifer reasoned. "You only knew him in high school. It's not the same thing. Knowing requires regular or at least occasional contact, like dating, talking, maybe a letter or two. Not years without so much as a hello."

"Gavin doesn't date," Leigh Ann told her, as though that were some kind of virtue.

"He does know how to talk. I heard him. Presumably he knows how to write. I understand he's written some songs. Can he dial a telephone?"

Leigh Ann looked at Jennifer as though she pitied her shallowness.

She had to restrain herself from reaching across the table and shaking Leigh Ann. The woman simply refused to get it.

"Exactly where have you been?"

"I told you. With Gavin."

"Specifics. Now. I dropped by your apartment, called you dozens of times, left so many messages on your answering machine—"

"I meant to speak to you about that. Don't you think you've been a little excessive? You and Teri ran out the entire tape—"

"Leigh Ann. I don't seem to be getting through to you. Ben Underwood is back in town." She was ashamed she'd said it even as the words left her mouth.

"So? He didn't bother anybody at the reunion, and I have Gavin to watch over me."

What she'd really wanted to say was that Danny had been murdered, but she couldn't. Not yet. Not without any proof. So she'd dropped back to their mother's old scare tactic. Seems it no longer worked on Leigh Ann. With Gavin by her side, she felt invincible.

"Your friend Gavin has written a song about Jimmy Mitch—"

"You heard it! So what do you think? My man has talent."

"Quit it!" Jennifer demanded, slapping her palm against the Formica tabletop. "Gavin might as well have taken out a full-page ad in the *Telegraph* saying 'Take your best shot.'

He's set himself up. In his song, he says Jimmy was murdered, and he threatens whoever killed him."

"Is that what you got out of it?"

Jennifer was exasperated beyond words.

Leigh Ann leaned forward. "Gavin can take care of me."

"And who's going to take care of Gavin?"

"We're fine. Really. We moved to another motel—" Leigh Ann put a hand over her mouth as though she'd let something slip that she shouldn't have.

Jennifer sat up. "Spill it. Why did you move?"

"The night of the reunion, we went back to his room to pick up some kind of equipment. He was planning to sing, you know. He has the most beautiful—"

"Leigh Ann . . ." Jennifer warned.

"Okay. Sheesh. You're *so* impatient. When we got there, he said something wasn't right. He does something when he leaves, puts a piece of paper or something between the door and the frame when he closes it, so he can tell if anyone has been in there. And sure enough, the paper was on the floor." She looked up at Jennifer from under her eyelashes. "It was no big deal. We didn't go in. He had the management remove his belongings."

"No big deal?" Jennifer exploded. "Tell that to someone who's standing next to the guy who catches the hand grenade."

"Calm down," Leigh Ann soothed. "No one has tried to harm us. Besides, I think it was just the maid."

It was like talking to a stone wall. In Leigh Ann's eyes, Gavin was hero material. In Jennifer's . . . well, she hadn't quite figured out exactly what Gavin was just yet.

"So that's why I didn't see you later at the reunion."

Leigh Ann nodded.

Jennifer peered through the glass walls and into the dark just out of range of the store's lights. It looked creepy. She didn't like it that people she couldn't see could see her, especially when someone she knew had just died. And when someone she cared about had just lost her mind.

"Couldn't you have at least gotten reacquainted with him before you . . . you took up with him?"

"I know all I need to know about Gavin," Leigh Ann informed her, gulping down her coffee. "Besides, Gavin insisted I move back to my apartment."

Jennifer cocked her eyebrow.

"Alone. A girl only has so many sick days. Look, Jen, if I'd wanted a lecture, I would have invited Monique, not you." She grabbed Jennifer's hand. "Can't you just be happy for me?"

It seemed like such a simple request, and it was what friends were supposed to do. But not under these circumstances. All of her motherly instincts were making her skin prickle, the same ones, she was sure, her own mother had felt when she'd told her she was going out with Danny Buckner. And the same ones that would jump all over her if her own daughter brought home a Gavin or a Danny.

"Won't he be going back to California soon?" Jennifer asked hopefully.

"Not if this deal goes through."

This was worse than she'd thought. "You mean Gavin might move back to Macon permanently?"

"Of course not, but for a while, at least until his career makes it necessary for him to leave."

Somehow this all seemed backward. Gavin should have started out in Macon, not be coming back here now. There had to be more to the story.

"Why'd he leave?" Jennifer asked.

"California?"

"No, Macon. Why'd he take off after high school? You were here, Phoenix Recording Studios was here, and we don't have earthquakes." A fact probably more of interest to Jennifer than to either Gavin or Leigh Ann. "Why'd he go? Don't pretend you haven't asked him."

The happiness drained from Leigh Ann's face. "He won't talk much about it, but what happened with Jimmy really hit him hard. They were—"

"First cousins," Jennifer finished.

"Right. How did you know?"

She shook her head. "Jimmy's probably living the high life in Las Vegas, never giving a one of us a second thought."

It was a fantasy of hers, created in the dark nights of her childhood. So why should she think Jimmy was dead now? Because a song Gavin wrote reminded her of Jimmy's disappearance? Maybe the song was simply one of Gavin's fantasies. She'd hate for anyone to believe what she wrote was true. She *was* overreacting, just like Leigh Ann kept telling her. Or so she hoped.

Leigh Ann nodded enthusiastically. "I told Gavin I thought Jimmy ran away, too. The kid couldn't stay out of trouble. His parents didn't seem all that surprised. He'd run off before. Only this time he didn't take anything with him, and he never came back."

"No word? Not ever?"

Leigh Ann shook her head. "Not even a postcard."

"Maybe there was some girl involved," Jennifer suggested.

"I don't think so," Leigh Ann assured her. "Jimmy didn't seem that far along socially."

"So what's Gavin think happened to him?"

"You heard the song. He thinks Jimmy's dead. That summer, all Gavin wanted was to get away from here."

"But he didn't leave," Jennifer pointed out, "at least, not until two years later."

"He couldn't. He was only sixteen, and his therapist—"

"Gavin was in therapy?"

"He took Jimmy's disappearance really hard. He had . . . well, he had a kind of breakdown. He spent over a month in the hospital. I went to visit him there once. I wasn't sure he even knew who I was. For a while they didn't think he'd be able to come back to school in the fall, but he did."

Jennifer nodded. Maybe writing that song was Gavin's way, however deranged, of dealing with Jimmy's ghost. Maybe the people he believed he was threatening didn't actually exist.

"Did you hear what happened at the reunion?" Jennifer asked.

Leigh Ann nodded. "We'd already left, but I caught it Sunday morning on the news. I tried to call you but I didn't get an answer, and I didn't want to leave a message on your machine." She touched Jennifer's hand. "I'm really sorry."

As though Danny's death were somehow her personal loss. In some way, she supposed, it was.

Headlights flashed through the window of the bakery as an old blue Chevy van with some kind of Hawaiian scene outlined with red hibiscuses painted on its side pulled up directly in front of the doors. The van lights went out and the driver's door opened. Gavin. She should have known. If she could have picked a vehicle for him, that would be it, but why was he here? Could it be a coincidence?

He strode in and walked directly to their booth, nudging Leigh Ann over as he sat himself down and slung one arm behind her. Then he propped both booted feet on the bench next to Jennifer, one entire knee exposed through the rip in his jeans.

He looked Jennifer straight in the face, his streaked blond hair hanging over his eyebrows, his clear blue eyes cold as ice.

"You girls shouldn't be out alone at night."

"And why not?" Jennifer bristled, not at all sure she cared to have Gavin Lawless telling her what to do. Or calling her a girl.

"They're killing people again," he said.

Chapter 20

"Excuse me?" It took Jennifer several seconds to process what Gavin had said, and even then she was sure she must have misunderstood.

"You heard me," Gavin insisted, dropping his feet to the floor and relaxing back against the booth.

"What do you mean? Who's been killed?" Jennifer asked, certain she already knew his answer.

He shrugged. "Suicide. Murder. What's the difference except in who gets the credit? The man's dead."

"So you think Danny Buckner was murdered." Believing that Danny was murdered was becoming an epidemic.

He looked at her with those crystal-blue eyes, cold as steel, but he didn't say anything. She could tell from his look that he didn't intend to.

She swallowed hard. "Who do you think killed him? And why?"

"If I knew who, do you think I'd be sitting in some bakery, watching out after two women who should be home in bed?"

"Then answer the why."

He shrugged.

It was all bluster. All speculation. He didn't know any more than she did, and she was irritated as heck she'd let him upset her. For all she knew, the man was still unstable.

"How could you think Danny Buckner's death has anything to do with Jimmy Mitchell's disappearance?" She waited for a response. "I heard your song."

"The title is 'Don't Forget.' Isn't it absolutely wonderful?" Leigh Ann gushed.

She knew she could count on Leigh Ann for an unbiased opinion.

"Why'd you send a copy to Sheena Buckner?" she asked when he still didn't answer.

"It's called promotion," Gavin said.

"Sheena was head of the reunion com—" Leigh Ann began.

"It's called baiting," Jennifer stated, totally ignoring Leigh Ann.

Gavin's mouth broke into a grudging smile. "Ya think?"

"It's a dangerous game," she reminded him.

"So, you want to play?"

She was actually in a staring contest, the kind that kids play in the third grade. Gavin had no intention of backing down, and she had no intention of letting him intimidate her.

"We're on the same side," she told him, searching his eyes. If Gavin had been afraid as a sixteen-year-old, he wasn't anymore. If only she could say the same for herself. She dropped her gaze. "I want to know why Danny got upset when he listened to it."

"So do I." Gavin suddenly seemed more interested in what she was saying.

"How do you know he heard it?" Leigh Ann asked.

"Sheena told me," Jennifer said.

"This isn't a good place to talk," Gavin said. "You girls need to get home. It's not safe to be out at night."

"It never has been," Jennifer pointed out much more

courageously than she felt, and wondering how safe it was to be out with Gavin.

"Is that why you're following Leigh Ann?" she demanded, suddenly realizing there was no way that Gavin could have just happened upon the place. It was a good distance from Leigh Ann's apartment, and definitely not one of Macon's hot spots. Which meant he had most likely tailed her to Monique's and then come after them here. He was either obsessive, paranoid, dangerous, or all of the above. She didn't expect him to answer her, and he didn't.

Jennifer wrapped her bear claw in a napkin and stuffed it into her purse. Something told her she wouldn't be interested in eating it for quite some time.

He shoved his hair out of his eyes and looked down at Leigh Ann, a soft look. "You ready?"

Leigh Ann moved over near him.

"Come on," he told Leigh Ann, taking her hand.

Obediently, she slid out of the booth, taking a final sip of her coffee.

"Oh, no you don't," Jennifer almost shouted. "You don't make accusations about people getting murdered and then just walk away."

The woman behind the counter quit shelving doughnuts and turned to stare.

Gavin gave Jennifer a look that made her stop. "I'm not talkin' to no hysterical female in no public place, so listen up. We'll follow you home, and then come back for Leigh Ann's car. That's the safest way." He didn't wait for her to agree.

She didn't particularly like Gavin or his attitude, but paranoia was an easily transmitted disease. She felt a shiver cross her shoulders. It was only a few blocks to her apartment building, and if he wanted to see her home—as long as Leigh Ann was with him—she didn't see the harm.

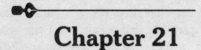

Chapter 21

Thank God Sam was waiting at her door when she got home. She had no desire to go into her apartment—or anywhere else for that matter—alone. Muffy was a courageous mutt, but dogs were no match for determined human beings.

His arm felt good around her as they cuddled on the sofa. She burrowed closer against his chest, closed her eyes and snuggled his neck.

Sometimes Sam could make the world go away. She wanted Gavin, his song, and all thoughts of murder, suicide, and vanishing out of her mind.

"Real nasty business," Sam whispered in her ear.

Her eyes popped open. Those were not the words she hoped to hear.

He leaned forward, pulling her with him, retrieved a bottle from the coffee table and took a swig of beer. He allowed himself no more than one a day, and then only if it'd been a particularly difficult day. His legs were propped on the table, and Muffy lay directly beneath them.

She looked at him. His tie was loose, his hair slicked back with a few dark strands brushing his eyebrow, just the way she liked it. He looked beat, almost as tired as April had earlier that night. He'd been working nonstop all weekend, and he was going to talk about it, about the body the police had found. It was on his mind and talking was his way of coping. The least she could do was listen, even if she'd had more of death than she cared for in the last few days.

"Could it have been an accident?" she suggested, pushing herself upright.

"Not unless the guy walked all the way out there, accidently shot himself square in the face, and then disposed of the gun. No car anywhere around, and he sure wasn't living there. Kudzu had grown up all over one side of the bungalow. Floor had rotted through in several places. No running water, no electricity. He was dressed in a coat and tie. Most likely had been dead a day, two at the most. The body hadn't deteriorated much."

"You still don't know who he is?"

"Nope. The gunshot to the face—which occurred postmortem, by the way—is going to make identification pretty difficult."

"Why don't they just run his fingerprints? You said he hadn't been dead too long."

"The fingertips were snipped."

Surely she hadn't heard him right. "As in cut off?"

He nodded.

"How in the world—"

"Most likely a bolt cutter."

She felt sick to her stomach. "Why would anybody go to all that trouble to make sure the body wouldn't be identified? This sounds like something I'd write, not something that happens in real life. I mean a killer is usually concerned with not getting caught, as opposed to keeping the victim's identity a secret. Why would he do that?"

Sam shrugged. "You tell me. You're the mystery writer."

She punched his arm. "So you think he was killed there, in the house?" Better to talk about location. She was getting far too graphic an image of the body.

Sam shook his head. "No blood to indicate it. They suspect he was dumped. Guess whoever did it didn't realize the place was scheduled to be torn down. The owner had gone over after church to give the place a look-see."

Someone else, worried tonight, would soon be mourning, assuming the police were able to identify him. At least he'd been found. Jimmy Mitchell hadn't been so lucky.

Why was she suddenly so sure that Mitchell was dead? Because Gavin Lawless said so? There was something about Gavin, something that seemed, well, sincere, for lack of a better word. He seemed so sane, so reasoned, so certain. At least when he didn't seem illogical and totally off the wall. But how could he be so certain Mitchell was dead? Unless he were somehow involved.

But what if Mitchell wasn't dead? Ben Underwood had called out to him at the reunion. Did he have reason to believe Jimmy was alive and in Macon?

What if someone had tried to kill Jimmy, only he didn't die, and he was back from the grave, back to seek revenge? And it was he who had—

She needed to get a grip.

"Ever hear of a guy named Jimmy Mitchell?" she asked casually.

Sam took another swig of beer and then looked over at her. "Why?"

Darn. Couldn't he, just once, answer a simple question?

"He disappeared about twelve years ago, might have been a runaway. He was sixteen."

Sam was from North Carolina. He'd been working for the *Telegraph* for the past five years. It was unlikely he'd know anything about it.

He set his beer down and pierced her with those blue eyes of his. "You're the third person who's mentioned that name to me in the last three days."

Snuggling had definitely lost all its appeal for the night.

"Who else?" she asked.

"One of the policemen out at that house. He said Mitchell disappeared around this time of year, on a night with a full moon, like the one we had Saturday. Weirds him out. He was just a kid when it happened, but Mitchell lived in his neighborhood. Said when he finds a body like that one, he half expects it to be ol' Jimmy, popping up again like something out of an episode of *The Twilight Zone*, slipped back through some burp in time."

Sam chuckled as if he thought such an idea was funny.

It wasn't. The idea sent chills through her. She felt as though she'd slipped through some kind of time warp back at the reunion and into a reality right out of a teen horror flick. Her body might be thirty years old, but her emotional state was currently closer to eighteen. She was scared, irrationally and thoroughly scared. If the body wasn't Mitchell's could it possibly be . . .

Sam took her hand, lightly drumming his fingers against her own, staring at the movement. He looked serious.

"Who else mentioned Mitchell?" she asked.

"One of the other reporters at the reunion. One of the guests said that some guy named Ben Underwood had shown up for the festivities."

"Right. I saw him there."

"When?"

"Early in the evening."

Sam nodded. "He wasn't around later when the police started questioning people."

"I'm not surprised. I imagine Underwood's had more to do with the police than he ever wanted to."

"You know him, then."

"Only by sight. He was Jimmy's best friend. When Jimmy

went out that night, the night he disappeared, he left with Ben."

"So the police assumed that Underwood knew what happened to Mitchell."

"Right."

"Was he a suspect?"

Jennifer shook her head. "I don't know. They never found any evidence of a crime. Ben stuck to the story that he dropped Jimmy off at the school that night."

"How do you know all this?"

"The police questioned kids at school. Everybody knew what was going on."

"One more thing," he said. "I checked in on the status of Danny Buckner with the coroner. He'd been drugged, all right, before the carbon monoxide got to him. That's not all that unusual with suicides. They take pills or alcohol and then slit their wrists or crank up the engine. Only . . ."

"Only what?"

"The drug they found in his system—it's not the usual choice."

"How so?"

"It was one of those date-rape drugs."

"Whoa! Why in the world would he have that? And why would he take it? Those drugs render a person unconscious, unable to function, and usually create memory loss when the victim wakes up. If it's what I think it is, it works really fast once it's been ingested?"

"Right. Why do you know so much about it?"

"I was thinking about using it in my next novel. It's common on college campuses. I'm amazed the toxicologist thought to look for it."

"He didn't, exactly. It's in the same family as Valium, only much more powerful. Valium shows up in a lot of suicides. I guess something in the screening must have tipped him to it. Why would Danny have it?" he asked.

Jennifer stood and started pacing, suddenly more awake than she'd been since Gavin had dropped his bombshell on her at the bakery. "This is really weird. I can't imagine anybody using something like that on himself."

"That's not all. The piece of plastic tubing that ran from the tailpipe to the window didn't have any fingerprints on it."

She stopped and stared at him. "Are you telling me—"

He shook his head. "Not necessarily. The D.A.'s office is still calling the death a suicide. Maybe the lack of fingerprints is simply a fluke. Who knows? There were fingerprints all over the car doors from the people who found him, but they didn't find any of Buckner's. Could be they were obscured—"

"Or could be the handles had been wiped, too," she pointed out, sitting back down.

"Are you all right?" Sam touched her cheek.

She shook her head. "Are you going to print any of this in the paper?"

"Not yet. It wouldn't be wise. The police don't need the press giving away everything they know."

"So what do the police think, the ones who are actually involved in the investigation?" She grabbed his face and forced him to look directly into her eyes. "Say the words," she demanded. "Say it. Tell me what they think."

He looked at her, a puzzled, worried expression on his face. "Why is this so important to you?"

What could she say when she didn't even know herself? She shook her head. Finally, she managed, "I need to know."

"They're leaving open the possibility that Danny Buckner was murdered," Sam said.

She let go of him and sank back into the couch. Sheena had said it. Gavin had said it. She'd said it. But not until Sam let the words pass his lips did it seem irrevocable. Someone had murdered Danny Buckner.

"What are the police doing about it?" Jennifer demanded, sitting back up.

"They pulled Underwood in for questioning. He was still there when I left," he looked at his watch, "maybe forty-five minutes ago."

"Why? Do they think he killed Danny?"

"They're just talking to him."

"They have to have a reason."

"They say he showed up at the reunion acting drunk."

"That's right. I saw him. He was calling out to Jimmy."

"Right. A security guard took a flask off of him."

"So what are they going to charge him with? Public drunkenness?"

"Not likely. That flask was full of tea."

"You mean—"

"That's right. Underwood wasn't drunk."

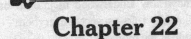

Chapter 22

Jennifer squinted at the early morning sun glinting off her windshield and tried hard to focus on her mission. It was time someone had a talk with Ben Underwood. Someone besides the police.

Last night she'd sent Sam home with an assignment: find every article about Jimmy Mitchell's disappearance that the *Telegraph* had ever printed. That paper stuck to the facts, at least as they knew them, unlike the *Atlanta Eye*. How Mitchell and Danny and Underwood could all be connected was anybody's guess, but she was beginning to think the old adage that there was no such thing as coincidence might just hold true.

Jennifer pulled her car, the dew still in the shadows, into the lot at the Best Western Motel on Riverside Drive. It'd only taken her a few minutes going down the motel listings in the yellow pages to find him. She thought it best to surprise Underwood early just in case he was thinking about cutting out of town.

Sheena pulled her Cherokee into the parking space right beside Jennifer's Bug, and confronted her as soon as they were both out of their cars. "What the heck is going on that you had to drag me out of bed before six o'clock in the morning?" The woman was a paragon of manners.

"Good morning to you, too. We're looking for Room

106," Jennifer told her, wishing she didn't have to bring Sheena along, but knowing she couldn't very well come by herself. Old fears died hard, especially hers. Sam would have a fit if he knew what she was up to.

She didn't know how Underwood fit into all this, only that he did. Gavin's rule—suspect everybody—seemed incredibly sensible at the moment.

"Why are we here?" Sheena demanded.

Jennifer shushed her. She had a voice that could wake, if not the dead, certainly the sleeping. "For once, trust me and don't ask questions. Let me do the talking."

Grumbling, Sheena followed her down the row of doors. The room was the next-to-the-last on the left. Just as Jennifer raised her hand to knock, the door swung inward and Ben Underwood stopped in front of her.

"What the—" he started.

"—Hell?" Sheena finished.

Jennifer swallowed hard. This had seemed a much better idea only seconds before. Underwood, ramrod straight, looked lean and tough, not to mention mean.

"Mr. Underwood, I'm Jennifer Marsh, and this is Sheena Buckner. We all went to high school together."

He stared at them, the muscles of his chest straining against the thin cotton of his olive-green T-shirt. "I think I remember her," he told Jennifer, "but you don't look familiar. Buckner. You related to that fellow that killed himself?"

Sheena nodded and Jennifer put a hand on her arm.

"I was sorry to hear about that," he said, bending to retrieve the morning newspaper.

Jennifer peered past him, into the room. He hadn't packed. Items were strewn here and there. He obviously didn't plan to go anywhere anytime soon. So the police hadn't scared him off. Or had told him to stay put.

"Actually, Sheena's husband, Danny, was murdered." Jennifer watched for a reaction. If he was surprised, he didn't show it.

"You don't say." For a moment he looked even meaner. He tapped the newspaper against his palm. "Is that what it says in here?"

She shook her head.

"You shouldn't forget that an attack of conscience can get to a man."

"That's not what happened," Jennifer insisted.

"Assuming you're right, do you two know what you're messin' with?" he asked.

At least he said "what" and not "who."

"We're not here to convince you that Danny was murdered," Jennifer told him, ignoring his question. "We simply need some information. You came back to Macon for a reason. I'm assuming you want to set the record straight about your involvement with Jimmy Mitchell's disappearance."

He stared at her. Leigh Ann was right. He didn't blink, at least not like normal people.

"I know you weren't drunk at the reunion Saturday night," she said. It was her trump card, the only one she had to play. "Why did you pretend you were?"

His eyes narrowed. Then he said, "Because I intend to find out."

"So do I."

"Find what out?" Sheena demanded, the time limit on her keeping quiet having just run out.

"Whether or not Jimmy Mitchell is really dead," Jennifer said.

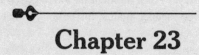

Chapter 23

Underwood invited them into his room, but no way was she going to step foot over that threshold. She knew not to take him back to her apartment, either. It was one of Johnny Zeeman's cardinal rules of criminal investigation: never let a suspect know where you live. Not that he couldn't find her address under J. Marsh in the phone book.

They settled on following his Saturn to the S&S Cafeteria a couple of blocks over. Besides, the restaurant made some of the best baking powder biscuits in town, and none of them had yet had breakfast.

They went through the serving line and then found a private corner in one of the smaller dining rooms. After they had transferred their dishes to the table, Sheena took the trays and stacked them on a nearby stand. The place wasn't all that full so early on a weekday morning.

Underwood stuffed his mouth with a huge bite of scrambled eggs mixed with grits. Then he mumbled around his food. "You can't get grits north of southern Virginia."

"I guess you've traveled a lot over the years with the Marine Corps," Jennifer suggested, splitting open a biscuit and slathering it with margarine from one of the little rectangle tubs, then topping it off with a heaping glob of blackberry jam.

He stopped chewing and cocked an eyebrow at her.

126

"I saw the base sticker on your bumper." That explained the haircut, the physique, the confidence, and why he knew the geographical boundaries for Southern food.

He bit off most of a slice of bacon and wiped the grease from his hands on a napkin.

"I heard what you said at the reunion. Do you really think Jimmy is still alive?" It was her personal favorite of all the possible solutions.

"You didn't know Jimmy, did you?" he asked, taking a healthy swig of orange juice.

She shook her head and watched as Sheena drowned her pancakes in brown-sugar syrup.

"He was a resourceful little guy. Kind of small for his age, but smart, wily, and honorable. To make me believe, you're going to have to show me some proof."

"He had a habit of running away."

"Right. He had issues but he wasn't a bad kid."

"But what about Gavin's song?" Jennifer said. "I'm assuming you heard it. I think he sent it to everyone he ever met. He seems convinced that Jimmy is dead."

"Gavin Lawson was a pothead who slept through most of the first two years of high school," Underwood stated. "When he wasn't high, he was drunk. Sometimes, he was both."

"You weren't friends, then."

"He was one of the best friends I've ever had. Doesn't change what he was."

"Did you . . ."

"Indulge? Nope. Never believed in it."

"What happened the night Jimmy disappeared?" Jennifer asked.

Underwood shook his head and then took a sip of coffee. "You didn't come to see me because you want to solve a twelve-year-old mystery. What's Jimmy got to do with Buckner?"

"We hoped you might be able to help us figure that out," Jennifer said.

He studied the two women before he spoke. She doubted he would tell them anything he hadn't told someone— at least the police—before, but she'd be grateful for even that much.

"Jimmy told his parents he was going out with me, but he wasn't."

"So you didn't see him that night." Sheena took a huge bite of pancakes.

"Of course I saw him. I picked him up at home and took him over to the high school."

"What time?"

"I guess it was close to ten o'clock."

"But he wasn't going to the dance," Sheena said.

"No."

"You mean you just dropped him and left?" Sheena went on.

He nodded.

"Where'd you go?" Jennifer asked.

"To a late movie and then to get something to eat."

"Alone?" Sheena asked, swirling a single bite of pancake in more syrup than Jennifer used on a whole stack.

"Alone," he assured them.

Leaving him totally without an alibi. Unless he had a ticket stub, and even then . . .

"He must have given you some kind of explanation for what he was doing," Jennifer insisted.

"He was meeting someone."

"At the prom? A girl?" Sheena asked.

Underwood shook his head. "I don't think so. This seemed more like business."

"What kind of business would a sixteen-year-old geek have to conduct?" Sheena asked.

His eyes narrowed and Sheena actually shrank back. Ben Underwood was not someone you insulted. Not anymore.

"He was going to tell me later."

"Okay, then tell us what he was going to get out of this business," Jennifer said. Sixteen-year-olds bragged. If Jimmy wouldn't say what he was doing, Jennifer suspected he couldn't resist telling why he was doing it.

"All he ever said was, it was a matter of honor."

"Honor?" Sheena almost choked on her food. "You've got to be kidding."

"How was he supposed to get home?" Jennifer asked, ignoring Sheena and hoping Underwood would do the same. Making light of honor to a Marine was not particularly wise.

"I was to come back to the school parking lot a little after midnight and wait for him."

"I take it he never showed up," Jennifer said.

Underwood shook his head. "The movie was long and I was a little late getting there. I waited and then finally went home about one. I figured he'd gotten another ride."

Maybe he had, and maybe that's why he was never seen again.

"Who were Jimmy's friends?" Jennifer asked.

"Mostly me and Gavin. The three of us hung pretty tight."

Sheena poked Jennifer with the back of her fork and yawned without bothering to cover her mouth. "This was some idea you had, Jenny. Getting me out of bed almost before daybreak and dragging me over here to talk about some kid who had nothing whatsoever to do with Danny—"

"I remember you now," Underwood told Jennifer. "She hated you." He pointed at Sheena. "She used to—"

"Right," Jennifer interrupted. "Ours is a complicated relationship."

"I'll bet."

"Ben, why does Gavin know so much?" Jennifer asked, kneeing Sheena and wishing she could stuff her under the table.

"I don't know. Jimmy must have told him."

"But when?"

"That's an excellent question."

"We're obviously missing something. You say Jimmy didn't have a girlfriend."

Ben shook his head.

"A crush, then," Jennifer suggested.

"Yeah, now that you mention it. There was a girl he talked about spending time with. A little redhead. Real cute. I think she was having trouble with her boyfriend at the time."

"Do you remember her name?"

He shrugged his shoulders.

"Sheena, you knew most everybody at school. Who were the redheads?"

"The only one who comes to mind right away is Candy Smyth, but she was a cheerleader—"

"That's right. She was on the cheerleading squad," Underwood insisted.

"No way," Sheena insisted, dropping her fork and pushing her plate away.

"You can't mean the Candy who married Al Carpenter?" Jennifer demanded.

"Yeah," Underwood agreed. "She must be the one. I know she was dating some guy on the football team."

"He drops a bombshell like that and you let him walk out of here?" Sheena asked, wadding her napkin and throwing it at Jennifer across the table. "You're pathetic, Jenny. You should have pumped him for details about Jimmy and Candy's relationship."

"I'd hardly call that a bombshell, and I doubt anyone other than you is interested in who was dating who back then," Jennifer snapped, tossing the napkin right back at her. "Besides, what did you expect me to do, physically restrain him? The man's a Marine. And what's wrong with you? You're the physical one."

"Just what do you mean by that crack?" Sheena demanded.

"Nothing. Let the man go. If he finds out something, I'm sure we'll hear about it. Anyway, I don't think he had anything to do with Jimmy's disappearance. Or with Danny's murder."

"You're too soft, Jenny, but that's just one of your problems."

"And you're not. That's one of *your* problems. He wasn't going to tell us any more than he already had. I've written enough of these scenes in my novels to know. We got all we could out of him."

"In your novels? Why don't you try visiting the real world now and then, Sherlock."

At the moment the real world held little appeal. It did, after all, contain one Sheena Cassidy Buckner.

"So what do you suggest we do now? Give up?" Sheena asked.

As if either one of them would.

"I want to know what the hell was all that about Candy being one of Jimmy's friends," Sheena demanded.

"Me, too. What say we give her an hour and then go ask her? Nicely," Jennifer added.

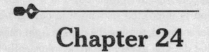

Chapter 24

Candy was clearing away her breakfast dishes when Sheena and Jennifer burst in upon her. Dressed in a thin blue cotton robe, she apologized profusely for throwing them out yesterday morning when her nerves had, as she put it, reached the frazzled stage. Then she ushered them to the kitchen table and offered to scramble up some eggs.

"No thanks," Sheena declined as Candy poured mugs full of hot coffee. "We just came from breakfast."

"I don't mean to be rude," Candy said, placing the mugs in front of them and joining them at the table, "but it's barely eight-thirty. The kids haven't been gone ten minutes." She pulled the robe tighter across her chest. "Has something happened?"

They'd come over and knocked on her door at that ridiculous hour, and Candy didn't want to be rude? Only in the South.

"What's this about you and Jimmy Mitchell being friends?" Sheena demanded, as though Candy had crossed some imaginary line. Never mind that the line had been drawn many years ago and that the person she had crossed it for was quite possibly dead.

Candy's eyes narrowed, and Jennifer sank back in her chair. If she was about to witness a cat fight, she didn't want to get hit with any flying fur.

But Candy's features softened and she said, "Whoever told you a thing like that?"

Jennifer nudged Sheena under the table, and Sheena scowled at her. "So it's not true."

"Jimmy was a nice boy. I didn't see the harm."

"Then you *were* friends," Jennifer said, leaning forward to block Sheena, suddenly defensive of a cheerleader who had broken the rules. She was liking Candy better all the time.

"I needed someone to talk to. Al and I were having problems and . . ." She shrugged. She couldn't confide in Sheena even all these years later. Why would anyone expect her to talk to her then? "Jimmy and I saw each other some."

"How about the night he disappeared?" Jennifer asked.

"Prom night?" Candy asked.

Jennifer nodded.

Her face reddened. "Al and I had had a fight earlier that day. We didn't go to the dance. Late that night I was with Sheena. We were . . ." Her eyes darted between the two women.

The toilet paper in the trees. "You were at my house," Jennifer stated.

"I'm really sorry about that, Jennifer." Candy dropped her gaze. "It was one of those crowd mentality things. I should never have let—"

"Cut the crap," Sheena interrupted. "You were angry as hell at Al."

"Consider it cut, *Sheena*." Candy rose up in her seat, and for a moment Jennifer was afraid she was going to reach across the table and grab a handful of hair.

"What time were you at my house?" Jennifer intervened.

"Maybe midnight," Candy offered, settling down.

"Could have been a little before," Sheena threw in.

It was some time after she'd called her father and before

they'd gotten home. Midnight was probably about right. Didn't take long to toss rolls of toilet paper over tree branches.

"What time did the two of you get together?"

Candy shrugged. "I don't know. What would you say, Sheena? About eleven?"

"That sounds about right. I ran into Candy outside the gym. After you and Danny left."

"But you were with Mick."

"We only went to the dance as friends. What did he care what I did the rest of the night?"

Maybe a lot.

"Did Jimmy ever ask you out?" Jennifer asked.

Candy stared at Sheena, a look of determination on her face. "Yes, he did."

"But you didn't go with him," Sheena insisted.

"No." Candy dropped her gaze. She seemed ashamed. Either because she was lying now to Sheena to save face or because she'd turned Jimmy down then for exactly the same reason.

"I was so angry with Al. I ran into him earlier outside the school, and we had another argument. He went looking for Jimmy."

"That night?"

Candy nodded.

"So he knew the two of you were friends."

"He wanted to find him, to beat him up."

"Why?"

"He thought I was at school to see Jimmy."

Underwood said Jimmy was meeting someone that night. Would he have been so foolish as to take Al on?

"Did he see him?" Jennifer pressed.

She shrugged. "I would never have married Al if for one moment I ever thought he had something to do with—"

"Where is that husband of yours?" Sheena asked.

"I . . ." Candy seemed to choke on her words. She cleared her throat. Her eyes searched theirs, her guard finally down. She looked truly frightened. "I don't know. I'm afraid. I'm worried that something may have happened to him. He's never been gone like this, not for days at a time without even a phone call."

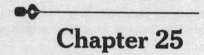

Chapter 25

Al had been the last known person seen with Danny Buckner. Where the heck was he? Jennifer had more than a few questions for him once he resurfaced. *If* he resurfaced.

At least she knew where Leigh Ann was. At work. Jennifer had checked as soon as she made it home from Candy's. Good. That should keep her away from Gavin and out of trouble for the next several hours.

Sheena, grumbling as though Candy had caused the collapse of her whole social structure, took herself off in her Jeep, fussing about the fact that Jennifer was abandoning her. But it was necessary. She couldn't take Sheena just anywhere, and where she planned to go next, Sheena would be a definite liability.

Ben Underwood had told them that Jimmy was meeting someone prom night, and Candy said Al had gone looking for him. That put Jimmy in direct conflict with at least one of Danny's group. The four of them were tight. They shared most things, even, on occasion, girlfriends. Mick had taken Sheena to the prom. Seth had dated Sheena and even asked Jennifer out once after she and Danny broke up. Surely at least one of them knew what Al had done that night—before and/or after he'd come knocking on the window of Danny's dad's old Chevrolet.

She could talk to Seth Yarborough, but he was investigating Danny's death, and if their lunch was any indication, he was unlikely to share what he knew or suspected with her. Where Al had got himself off to was anybody's guess. She hoped her guess was wrong. That left Mick Farmer, now sole proprietor of Macon Pictures.

Too bad she couldn't simply go see him on her own. But she didn't dare arouse his suspicions. As Gavin put it, somebody was "killing people again," and until she knew who, everyone was suspect. That pesky paranoia was rearing its ugly head.

She tapped her foot impatiently against the brake pedal of her Beetle. The appointment was for two o'clock. At 2:02 Teri finally showed up.

"You're late," Jennifer told her in the parking lot.

"Excuse me? You call me at 9:45 on a Tuesday morning, tell me to take the afternoon off from work and get myself over to some business I've never heard of, in a part of town I'm not that familiar with, for a meeting you made without once consulting me, and then you have the nerve—"

When she put it that way . . . "Sorry. I'm an insensitive clod and I deserve an unbridled tongue lashing. Only later. We've got to get inside. I told the receptionist it was vital that you see Mick today."

"Because?"

"I was hoping you'd come up with something on the way over here."

"Might have helped had I known I needed to." Teri tapped her foot. She could have such an attitude at times. "Now what exactly are we trying to find out?"

"I explained all that to you over the phone." At least as much as was possible about Jimmy and Danny and Al and Ben as a three-minute phone call would allow. Everything except her suspicion that Danny was murdered.

"Seems to me you've never quite gotten over high school, Jen. Let it go. What happened to Jimmy Mitchell is ancient history, unless . . ."

"Unless what?"

"Unless you think that's why Danny killed himself."

The words made her stop. She would be dishonest if she denied it hadn't occurred to her. The timing was right. Al had come to get Danny, and they had done what? She didn't want to think about it. Surely Danny wouldn't have harmed Jimmy or anybody else. Not her Danny.

"That's not what I think," Jennifer assured her, wishing she could leave all of the who-did-what-to-whom of her teenage years behind her. All she really wanted to know was who had murdered Danny.

Jennifer shuffled Teri past the glass door at the front of the building, hoping a little flattery might take some of the edge off Teri's bite. "You're so good at plotting," she said. "This should be easy as—"

"Can I help you, ladies?" The receptionist, clad in a summer floral dress, accosted them with a honeyed voice, which, no doubt, made her worth at least half her salary for just answering the phone.

"We're here to see Mr. Farmer."

"You must be his two o'clock." The woman glanced up at the clock on the wall—which was a full five minutes fast—and then back down at them. Jennifer shot a pointed look at Teri.

"Sorry. We're a little late," she confessed.

"That's all right," the receptionist beamed, apparently mollified by the apology. "Have a seat. I'll see if I can find him." Then she disappeared down a hallway.

"Now, exactly who is this dude?" Teri asked.

"Danny's business partner."

"And we're here because?"

"I want to know how they got along, if there was any ill will between the two of them."

"Uh—uh—uh," Teri warned. "Looking for a reason Danny killed himself will only bring you grief. Anyone with emotional baggage so big that he would—"

"Look. Don't worry about it. You've got a video project. That's all you need to know."

"What kind?"

"Anything you want. Make something up or use one of the plots from your novels—"

"And risk plagiarism? I guard those plots with my life."

"Okay, then. Just get us in the door, and I'll take it from there."

"Lord have mercy, Jennifer. The things I do for you."

"I know, and I love you for it."

"What did you tell the woman when you made the appointment?"

"Just that you're an independent filmmaker, and you're going to be needing some professional services. But not really. Remember, whatever you do, don't sign anything."

"Maybe we don't need them now, but what if we filmed one of your mysteries, or better yet, one of my romances? Independent films are coming into their own. Everybody in America saw *The Blair Witch Project*. If the biggies in New York caught our stories in the theater . . ." Teri's voice dropped off as her gaze rose upward, and Jennifer turned.

He was medium height with dark hair flirting with his shoulders, eyes so brown they looked black, and skin tan enough to confirm the rumors floating around Riverside High that he had Native American blood somewhere in his lineage. His jeans were worn, but his white dress shirt, open at the throat, sleeves rolled to his elbows, looked new.

"Mick Farmer," he said, offering Teri his hand.

Farmer hadn't lost his appeal. He was having a definite drool effect on Teri. Not good. Teri couldn't concentrate on two things at one time, and she was checking out the absence of a wedding band on Farmer's left hand a little too closely.

"You must be Ms. . . ."

"Teri. Call me Teri," she said, standing to accept his hand. *Focus.* Jennifer willed her thoughts to her friend.

Mick took a double take in Jennifer's direction.

"Hey, Mick. How ya been?" she asked.

"Fine," he said automatically. Then he shrugged his shoulders.

"I'm really sorry about Danny," Jennifer offered. "I'm sure it's been hard on you and the business. Is Sheena helping out?" She didn't see how she had time, but she wanted his reaction.

"Sheena?" He frowned.

"Yes. I thought, now that Danny's gone, she might—"

His look stopped her cold. "Might what?"

"Be helping out here."

"Oh." He shrugged. "That actually might not be a bad idea. I suppose I could train her if she wants back into the business." He gave her a funny look. "Have you and Sheena . . ."

She shook her head. "I was just curious."

"Are the two of you together?" He pointed at Teri.

Jennifer nodded. "I'm here for moral support."

"Well, then, why don't you come back to my office and tell me what it is we can do for you."

They followed Mick into a good-sized room where he pulled out chairs for them around a small table near the window.

Jennifer scanned the room. The only photo on his desk showed a big black Lab on a boat, the wind whipping its fur.

"I believe you told my secretary you had some footage you want us to work on for you."

"Right," Teri said, raising one eyebrow in Jennifer's direction.

"Want to tell me about it?"

Teri's face went blank.

"Personal, documentary, fictional?" Mick suggested.

"Fictional."

He made a note on a yellow legal pad. "Complete?"

"Not yet."

"So what are we looking at?" He paused, but Teri didn't say anything. "Timewise, I mean. How long is it?"

"Oh. An hour and a half sounds good."

"Is that in raw footage?" He scribbled a note on a pad.

"Probably not," Teri suggested, frowning at Jennifer. "I mean, that's the length I'm planning for the end product," recovering maybe a little too confidently.

He pursed his lips and nodded, then dropped his pen and leaned back, cocking his chair, with his hands behind his head. "Tell me about it."

"You mean—"

"Tell me the plot."

"I don't think that's necessary," Jennifer said.

"Sure it is," Mick insisted.

A look of panic flashed over Teri. This was not good, not good at all. She hadn't really had much time to prepare.

"It's a horror flick," Teri said, settling back into her chair. "A quasidocumentary."

She was going to describe *Blair Witch*, Jennifer thought. Not a bad idea.

"About a boy who disappeared . . ."

Definitely *Blair Witch*, Jennifer prayed.

". . . right here in Macon. On prom night."

Farmer let his chair legs drop back onto the floor.

Jennifer sat paralyzed, unable to speak, blink, or stuff a sock in Teri's mouth.

Teri leaned forward, warming to her subject. "A lot of it is filmed at night so it's got this dark, moody atmosphere."

"I see. Could make editing difficult."

"Of course, the interviews with the locals about the disappearance will be in the daylight. You look about the right age to remember what happened. Maybe you'd care to give me an interview."

He shook his head. "I'm strictly a behind-the-camera kind of guy." He tossed his pen down on the table and looked her in the eye. "Why are you doing this?"

His words echoed Jennifer's thoughts, but her *this* had a different reference.

Teri didn't even blink. "I want to know what happened to Jimmy Mitchell."

So much for subtlety.

Mick pursed his lips and looked straight at Jennifer. "What the hell are you up to?"

If Mick had been the silent, brooding type in high school, he'd definitely gotten over it.

Jennifer sat up in her chair. "Mick, Sheena thinks Danny was murdered. So do I."

"Murdered?" He said the word as though the idea surprised him, but she sensed it didn't.

"I thought I told you—" Teri began, but Jennifer cut her off.

"Whether Danny's death was a suicide or not, the catalyst appears to have been Gavin Lawless's song suggesting Jimmy was killed the night of our senior prom."

He must have heard the song—who hadn't?—but he didn't react to her mention of it.

"Tell me what you remember of that night, Mick," Jennifer said. "Al came and got Danny out of the car where we were parked near the school's loading dock. He said he needed his help. Did he come get you, too?"

Mick shook his head. "I was with Sheena."

"No," she insisted. "This was later, sometime after Seth had been crowned prom king. Sheena made a scene trying to get Danny to dance with her. He shrugged her off. You tried to distract her, and we left. Sheena told me the two of you parted company shortly after that."

He sat there not saying a word.

"Talk to me, Mick," Jennifer pleaded. "What did you do?"

"I went home. What else does a guy do when his date ditches him?"

She felt like shouting, *Get over it! That was twelve years ago,* but she knew better. "Did you see Jimmy at all that night?"

"Yeah. I saw him earlier, arguing with Al."

"When?"

"I don't know exactly. Sheena had to go to the rest room, so I stepped outside for a smoke. I heard a couple of guys getting loud by the trees. One of them was Al. I think the other one was Jimmy. Candy stepped in between the two of them."

"Candy?"

"Yeah. I heard her tell the other guy to go on and he backed away. Then she and Al walked away together, but he was none too happy about it."

"How do you know?"

"She tried to hold his arm, but he pulled out of her grip. He was drunk."

"How do you know that?"

"Al was always drunk." Mick stood up and slid back his chair. "Let me give you both a little free advice: let it go."

"Why?"

"You tell me. You're the one who thinks Danny was murdered."

Chapter 26

What was she going to do with Teri?

"Way to tell everything you know. Are you out of your mind?" Jennifer demanded in the parking lot of Macon Pictures. "Now he knows what we're looking into."

"Excuse me? Did I not tell you to drop this whole Danny-was-murdered theory Saturday night?" She sniffed. "You opened your mouth, and I suppose everything you ever knew about prom night at Riverside High School just happened to fall out."

Teri was being totally unfair, and Jennifer would tell her if she could get a word in.

"I don't know what you're so upset about," Teri rushed on. "He told you what he knew. Besides, we got some in-your-face, immediate shock-reaction data. Jimmy Mitchell makes him nervous and Sheena Buckner makes him hot. I just hope he's not too focused on the young widow. That fine hunk of male attitude was too cool for words."

"What we got was a warning, and you're sounding way too much like Leigh Ann."

"Surely you couldn't be suspicious of a guy as good-lookin' as that." Teri sniffed, then added, "Don't compare me to a woman who regularly gets neck strain checking out babes as she walks down the street."

"Of course I'm suspicious, and why not? Leigh Ann is

your very good friend, and you would do well to remember it."

"Duh and duh. You're good at rewriting history, Jennifer. You know that?"

"Just go," Jennifer insisted, pushing Teri behind the steering wheel of her car and shutting the door behind her. She wanted Teri out of there and somewhere safer.

"You're upset because Mick scared you. He didn't threaten you. There's a big difference," Teri reminded her out her car window.

Jennifer nodded. "Whatever you say." As she turned toward her Beetle, she thought she caught an almost imperceptible movement of the blinds from the lobby of Macon Pictures. It had to be the air conditioner. Or her paranoia.

What the heck did she think she was doing? All she'd accomplished so far was to establish that everyone she ever knew or heard of was in the vicinity of Riverside High School prom night twelve years ago. Big surprise. She could have predicted that on her own.

Even if by some miracle she figured out what happened to Jimmy, she still wouldn't know what that had to do with Danny's death. She needed to put it all away for a while, to let her mind rest. She couldn't come up with one more original thought if her life depended on it.

Jennifer couldn't wait to get home and into her old baggy jeans, out of her shoes, and back into the pretense of a normal life. She'd left her detective in a most precarious position at the end of chapter two, and there was only one way for him to get out of it: she had to write it.

At least with her work, she had some control, and at the moment, control was the major element lacking in her own life.

*   *   *

Jennifer stared at her computer screen. She was no further than two chapters into her new novel about Zimmerman, a boozer of a private eye who had hit the wagon to help the long and luscious young thing who had flowed into his office on the second worst day of his life. She hadn't typed more than two sentences, and she'd been at it for more than thirty minutes. At the moment, murder was the last thing she wanted to think about.

Maybe she could work on the romantic element. She'd promised Zimmerman if he solved the case, she'd let him get the girl, but even she wasn't buying that idea. She should have made this guy more attractive. A few searches and deletes could get rid of that bald spot in the back of his head. She could take away that smoker's hack, get some of the grime off his office windows, and maybe—

The phone rang, and she snatched it up. It was Leigh Ann having one of her little fits. "Calm down," Jennifer insisted. "I can't understand a word you're saying." She could hear loud heaves and then the phone hitting something hard.

"Leigh Ann?" she called into the receiver.

No response.

"Leigh Ann," she called louder, a hint of panic replacing her annoyance. "Answer me. If you don't say something in the next five seconds, I'm calling 911."

"Okay, I'm back," Leigh Ann said. Her breathing, a little more regular, was still audible. "I had to get a glass of water."

Was that all? "Okay, good. Now try telling me what happened. Slowly," Jennifer suggested. Whatever brilliant revelation she'd been about to commit to her hard drive had flown right out of her head.

"It blew up!" Leigh Ann said.

Jennifer clicked on Save and then Close. Leigh Ann, for all her bluster, had never used the words "blew up" before.

"Now what are you talking about? You can't possibly mean a bomb."

"If he hadn't become suspicious and dived out of the driver's seat of his van . . ." She panted even harder. "God, Jennifer. He could have been killed. Or maimed. Or . . . Oh, Lord, what if he hurt his hand?"

"Who?" Jennifer demanded, just to make sure.

"Gavin. Who did you think I was talking about?"

"How seriously was he hurt?"

"I don't know. He called me from Macon General. He has some scrapes on his head and his arms. He rolled under a nearby car and it shielded him somewhat from the explosion."

"If he called you, he can't be that bad off, so settle down. Was anybody else hurt?"

"No. I don't think so."

Thank goodness for that.

"Are they keeping him?" Jennifer asked.

"You mean in the hospital?"

"Did he give you a room number?"

"No. He was leaving. He's got to get some kind of transportation and find a safe place to stay. Before he hung up he said something else."

"What?"

"He told me not to talk to you anymore. He doesn't trust you, Jennifer."

Well, she didn't trust him, either, and now he was undermining Leigh Ann's trust in her. He could readily have blown up his own van, although she had to admit that would be a major sacrifice, considering the art work on the side. At least it would take the suspicion off him.

"So. Are you going to listen to him?" She held her breath.

"If you hadn't noticed, I called you. So don't start preaching to the choir."

Go, Leigh Ann. That was her girl.

"Does he have any idea who might have done it?" Jennifer asked.

"Nope. But he's pretty sure why. I take it you haven't seen this morning's copy of the *Atlanta Eye*."

"It's Tuesday, Leigh Ann. The *Eye* doesn't come out until Wednesday."

"They put out a special edition dedicated to Macon."

Oh, great. What had Teague done now? "Break it to me gently."

"Half of the front page has to do with what happened at the reunion. There's a huge picture of Sheena and Mary Jo going at it over the crown, and a smaller inset photo of Danny's graduation picture. It's kind of grainy so I bet they lifted it from the yearbook. The headline reads: 'Prom Queen Struggles Over Past Jealousies While Husband Kills Himself in Parking Lot.' "

"They got all that on one line?"

"Three, actually. Inch-high letters. Most of the text of the article is inside. The lower half of the page has a big picture of Gavin playing his guitar. His headline reads: 'Song Holds Key to Long-Ago Disappearance.' "

She didn't bother to ask whose byline the articles had come out under. Teague had come to Macon on Sunday morning for an interview with guess who. Well, there was only one surefire cure for stupidity, and it looked as though someone had tried to apply it to Gavin.

"I want you to promise me you'll stay away from Gavin, at least for a while."

"You know how unfair it is for you to ask me."

"I do."

"He needs me right now, Jennifer."

"I know. But he needs you alive. Promise me."

There was a long pause.

"Don't make me come over there," Jennifer threatened.

"Okay, okay."

"Don't go anywhere, not even the grocery store, without calling me first. Understand?"

"Yes, Mama Jen."

"There's nothing we can do except let the police investigate."

If Gavin wanted to get himself killed, that was one thing, but he'd better not do anything to endanger Leigh Ann.

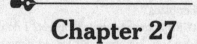

Chapter 27

Sam offered her a single white rose when she opened the door to his knock at six o'clock. It was her first break from staring at her computer screen since Leigh Ann's phone call. She couldn't work, only pretend. Danny was dead, Gavin had been attacked, and she didn't know what to do about it.

"What's the occasion?" she asked, noticing the fresh haircut, the crisp shirt, pressed tie and jacket, and scent of aftershave. He must have taken off work a little early, gone home, showered, and changed. He was looking *really* good. "Did we have a date?"

"Yes, only you didn't know about it. We have a reservation for seven-thirty. I thought you could use a little dinner and maybe some dancing."

Oh, he was being good. Very good. Sam didn't dance, and she loved to. It was probably the only offer she couldn't refuse, and he knew it, because he never would agree to go. But that didn't keep her from trying.

"Where?"

"At that new club on Zebulon Road, Casablanca."

The one she really wanted to see inside. She'd passed it on the way to the movie theater. It had a tropical theme and looked enticingly exotic. But . . .

"I'm a mess." She ran her hand through her hair. It really needed washing.

"A gorgeous mess."

More than good. He had just upgraded himself to great. "And I have other plans."

"To do what? Sit home and write? Or fret? I don't think so." He pulled her into his arms and leaned down, gazing into her eyes. "Come tango with me into the night."

She giggled. A tango with Sam would no doubt be more of a tangle. Besides, she couldn't tango either, and she was sure the musicians at Casablanca were not the tango type.

He kissed her nose. "So what do you say? Have I sweet-talked you enough? Let's blow this joint."

Muffy, who'd been biding her time waiting for her turn at attention, wedged her nose between the two of them.

"If you won't dance with me, I'm sure Muffy will."

Upon hearing her name, Muffy let out a loud woof and vigorously wagged her tail.

"See? I told you."

Draping her arms over his shoulders, she kissed his neck. "I'd love to," she whispered into his ear, taking a quick nip at his earlobe. She felt him shudder. It'd be nice if for once they could call an evening their own.

She broke away. "But I'm sort of watching Leigh Ann long-distance."

"Why are you baby-sitting Leigh Ann?"

"The woman can't be left alone. Only she won't let me stay with her. I don't want to go into all the details. Okay?" Thankfully, Leigh Ann had broken Gavin's trust, but she wouldn't.

If Sam was curious, he let it pass. "Understood. Let me offer a solution. We'll leave her my pager number. That way you can go out, have fun, and still fulfill your friendly obliga-tions. Besides, that information you wanted me to get for

you, the *Telegraph*'s accounts of Mitchell's disappearance—
I've got it."

He was even better than she thought. Only he was playing
his hand a little fast.

"Where?" Playfully, she searched his pockets.

He wrapped his arms around her, pinning hers. "No, no,
no, my dear. Dinner first. Then dancing. And if you've been
exceptionally good at relaxing, information for dessert."

Who cared about dessert? She could stay like that, with
Sam's arms about her, forever. As long as forever was no
longer than twenty minutes. She had to get dressed, and she
knew exactly what to wear: a shimmery, midnight-blue cock-
tail dress that had been gathering dust in her closet for six
months and still had the tags on it. Now if she could only
figure out what the heck she was going to do with her
hair . . .

The food was wonderful. She'd have to tell Dee Dee to
check out the honey butter they served with the freshly
baked loaf bread. It had an extra ingredient, something she
couldn't quite put a name to, but Dee Dee would know.

The dancing—at least Sam's version, which had more to
do with planting his feet in one spot and swaying back and
forth, so, according to him, he couldn't step on her feet—
was heavenly.

Unfortunately, her curiosity kept rearing its ugly head.
She wanted to know what he'd found out, but every time
she mentioned it, he pressed his finger to her lips and said,
"Over dessert or not at all."

Sheeesh. He could be *such* a drag.

But by the time she'd finished her second glass of wine,
Sam's eyes were getting deeper and bluer all the time. She
didn't much remember what it was she wanted to know.

"Two almond cheesecakes," Sam ordered, handing the

menus back to the waiter. "Plus two coffees. Make hers decaf. Better yet, bring the pot." He studied her face. "Your eyes have dilated to an alarming degree."

"Thanks for noticing." She could feel them contract as he said the words. Sam had an uncanny talent for breaking moods. "So spill it. Dessert's officially on the way."

"I didn't find much more than what you'd already told me in the newspaper accounts of Mitchell's disappearance, but I did talk to Harry Osner."

Her gaze followed the swirl of red liquid as she rotated the stemmed glass. As his words registered, she threw him a puzzled look.

"The guy whose byline is on all the stories," Sam explained.

Ah, yes. Print the whole story, except for the part that might get you sued. Maybe, just maybe, Sam had learned something. She leaned forward.

"He never spoke directly with Underwood—they kept him pretty well shielded—but Osner was tight with the investigating officer." He sipped his wine.

Thirdhand information, but she'd take what she could get and hope they weren't all playing a game of telephone. "Yeah, and . . ."

"He said young Ben was scared."

"Of course he was scared, being dragged in for questioning by the police."

Sam shook his head. "Sure he was frightened of the police and the whole situation, but he refused to talk. No matter what they threatened him with."

"You mean . . ."

"Right. He may have been afraid of the police, but he was either petrified they'd learn something he'd done, or a whole lot more afraid of someone else."

"So you think he'd been threatened?"

"Maybe not directly. But I think we can be pretty sure, one way or the other, Underwood never believed Mitchell ran off. And neither did the police."

Jennifer put down her glass. "Ben didn't come back to school that year. He was home-schooled for the remaining month. We all thought it was because of all the gossip."

"When in fact it may have been—"

"Because he didn't feel safe."

"Right."

"But he did graduate on time, right?"

Sam nodded. "He was back in regular classes come fall."

"Did Osner mention Gavin—" Jennifer began, but Sam's pager let out a series of beeps.

He pulled it out and looked. "It's Leigh Ann. Her number plus 911."

"That means it's serious."

Simultaneously, they pushed back from the table and stood up at the same moment their cheesecake arrived. Jennifer gave it a look of regret.

"Enjoy," Sam told the waiter, patting his shoulder and dumping a wad of bills on his tray.

And then they were gone. Leaving the waiter with his mouth open and his hand in the air.

Chapter 28

Leigh Ann must have been watching out the window of her ground floor apartment, because she was out the door and into the parking lot as soon as Jennifer and Sam drove up. Her building was at the extreme back of the complex. It offered privacy. In this case, maybe a little too much privacy.

Leigh Ann's car, a hatchback coupe, stood half in and half out of a parking space, blocking access to the back part of the lot. Sam pulled his Honda against the curb near a stand of pine trees and cut the engine.

Leigh Ann was at the passenger side door before Jennifer could even get it open. "Something's wrong with my car," she sputtered.

"I don't do cars, and I suspect Sam doesn't either," Jennifer reminded her, perturbed that their first evening out in more time than she could remember had been interrupted by a summons to Leigh Ann's apartment. She was obviously all right. No blood, fire, flood, or mayhem. She'd given up cheesecake and Casablanca and Sam playing-it-again for a broken automobile? Leigh Ann should have called AAA.

But when she caught a better glimpse of her friend's face . . .

"What is it? What happened?" Jennifer demanded, a hollow feeling settling in the pit of her stomach. She pushed open the door, got out, and grabbed Leigh Ann by the shoulders.

"I know you told me not to go out at night, but I was only going to be gone for just a second. To the drugstore. I started to back my car out of the parking space. It wouldn't stop when I stepped on the brake pedal. I bumped the car parked in the row behind me."

"Okay." She let go of Leigh Ann. "So why was it again that we had to get over here so fast?"

"Did you check your brake fluid?" Sam asked, coming up beside them.

"Yeah. It's all over the asphalt."

Light was dawning in her poor brain, if a little slowly. "Where?" Jennifer asked.

They followed Leigh Ann, who was shivering as though it was much cooler than it actually was, to the space in front of her car.

"There." Leigh Ann pointed to two puddles of reddish brown liquid.

Both Jennifer and Sam bent down, touching it. Sam rubbed it between his fingers and smelled it. She hoped he knew what brake fluid looked like because she had no idea. Whatever this was, it obviously should have been in something, not lying on the ground.

"Do you mind getting me a flashlight from the trunk? And see if I left that brown tarp in there." Sam offered her his keys.

By the time she got back with the light and the tarp, he had his coat and tie off and his sleeves rolled to the elbow. He pushed on Leigh Ann's car to make sure it was level and not about to move, unfolded the cover, shoving it as best he could under the frame, and then carefully shimmied under the front part of the coupe.

There went his shirt, possibly his trousers, and definitely

the evening. Leigh Ann was going to owe her big-time for this one.

"What do you see?" Leigh Ann bent down and called under the side of the car.

Jennifer watched the flashlight beam flick out and about from under the car.

"Are you finding anything?" Leigh Ann asked.

"More fluid." Sam's voice sounded muffled.

"Where's it coming from?" Jennifer added, but he didn't answer. They could hear him shifting against the asphalt, and the foot that hung out on their side disappeared.

In another few seconds he rolled out on the other side. Before he'd even gotten back on his feet, Leigh Ann was all over him. "What'd you find?"

"We need to stay calm," Sam said, as much for her benefit as for Leigh Ann's. "I want you to go inside and call the police."

"But why should—"

"Your brake line's been cut."

Leigh Ann stared at him, obviously confused. "It couldn't—"

Sam grabbed her by the shoulders, and for a moment Jennifer thought he was going to shake her. "Don't go into denial on me. That's why you called us. You suspected it might have been cut. Otherwise, you would have called a garage."

"God. Somebody just tried to kill me." Apparently Leigh Ann's knees went to jelly, because she dipped slightly. Jennifer steadied her. Now if only someone would steady her.

"The brake line's been severed at each of the wheels," Sam told them.

"Maybe they're just old," Leigh Ann insisted. "Maybe they wore—"

"Clean slices. Not worn, not ragged, but sliced. As in cut."

Jennifer's breath caught in her chest. She didn't dare breathe. Surely he was wrong. Surely, somehow, he was mistaken.

She searched Sam's face. Even in the light of the streetlamp she could tell he was dead serious.

Whatever madness was sweeping Macon had just got even more personal, and Jennifer didn't appreciate it one bit. She'd already lost one friend. She wasn't about to lose another. She had to stay calm. And rational.

"Where's Gavin?" Jennifer asked.

"At his motel, I'm sure. He said he didn't want to put me in danger. Oh, my."

Sam took them each by the elbow. "Let's get inside."

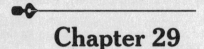

Chapter 29

The police took the report, examined the car, asked who might want to hurt her, and told Leigh Ann to be careful. Jennifer hadn't expected more. After all, what could they do?

"They didn't even offer me the witness protection program," Leigh Ann grumbled.

"I'm sure it was an oversight," Sam assured her, his white shirt grimy and his hair a mess.

Jennifer was trying hard not to be angry with Leigh Ann, not to go into her what-were-you-thinking-hooking-up-with-a-guy-you-hardly-know mode, because somewhere deep in her gut, she couldn't help but put some of the blame on Gavin. Not because she should, not because he was responsible, but because she felt certain his association with Leigh Ann had somehow put her in the line of fire.

Preaching at Leigh Ann wouldn't help. She was already sufficiently rattled. Or so Jennifer hoped.

They sat at the small glass-and-metal table near the window of the tiny kitchen area, drinking the coffee that Jennifer had made. Leigh Ann got up once more and adjusted the blinds, making sure that no one could see in.

"Gavin has stirred up something he should have left alone," Jennifer said, not able to keep her thoughts to herself.

"Gavin Lawless? What's he got to do with—" Sam asked.

"He's Leigh Ann's old high school boyfriend," she told Sam, as though that explained it.

"You're not being fair," Leigh Ann insisted. "Gavin's not to blame. And he's my current boyfriend, Jennifer. Gavin's the one who said Danny was murdered, remember?" Leigh Ann reminded her. "He told us in the bakery that 'they're killing people again.' He wouldn't have said that if he was the one doing the killing. He didn't do anything to Jimmy, and he certainly didn't do anything to Danny. I was with him every minute the night of the reunion, remember?"

"Whoa, whoa, whoa," Sam interrupted. "What's this about killing people again?"

She hated it when people walked in late on a movie or a conversation, and this wasn't much different. Whatever she said, she'd be sure to leave out something vital.

"Gavin thinks Jimmy Mitchell, the boy who disappeared twelve years ago, was murdered. That's what his song is about," she explained patiently. "He seems to think whoever did in Jimmy had a hand in what happened to Danny."

"I see. Well, for what it's worth, I don't think anyone was trying to kill you," Sam told Leigh Ann.

"But her brake lines!" Jennifer said. He was the one under that car. Had he not said—

"Calm down," Sam told her.

Telling Jennifer to calm down was as good as using a poker on a fire. He put a hand over hers.

"Look at this rationally. Leigh Ann couldn't even get out of the parking lot," Sam reminded her. "This seems more like a warning."

A warning. Two in one day.

"If someone really wanted to do her harm, they'd wait

until the car was parked on the street, preferably on a slope."

"Do I look like somebody who needs to be warned?" Leigh Ann demanded.

Jennifer grabbed her with her free hand. "Of course not." But someone else had, assuming *that* someone hadn't cut the lines himself. She turned to Leigh Ann. "You weren't with Gavin every minute at the reunion. We first saw him after I talked with Danny."

"How long after, and why would you think Gavin had something to do with Danny's death?" Sam asked.

"A while, and because I think his stirring up trouble over Mitchell's death is the reason Danny was murdered."

"Is not," Leigh Ann declared in a huff.

"It would have taken a while for the murderer to drug Buckner and set up that car, but the actual time it took the carbon monoxide to—"

"Please," Jennifer interrupted.

Sam took another sip of coffee from the Macon Whoopee Ice Hockey mug that Leigh Ann had set out for him. "What is it you think Gavin had against Buckner?"

"Nothing," Jennifer stated, "but I think Danny may have somehow walked into the line of fire."

"You know something, Jennifer?" Leigh Ann's face was solemn, and Jennifer could tell she was about to get ugly. "You talk about me being in denial, but I think there's a really simple solution to everything that's happened. You won't admit it because you don't want it to be that way."

"Go on," Sam urged.

"Danny killed himself because he was involved with Jimmy's disappearance. Gavin's song drove it home to him that people weren't going to forget about that kid who vanished."

She'd stopped short of saying Danny might have killed

Jimmy, and for that Jennifer was grateful. She wouldn't be honest if she denied the thought hadn't crossed her own mind, but she'd rejected it, and for good reason.

"Fine," Jennifer agreed. "Let's assume Danny killed Jimmy and somehow disposed of his body while, I might add, he and I were wrestling in his dad's old Chevrolet on prom night."

Sam shot a questioning look her way, but she didn't have time to deal with his curiosity right now.

"Then who, exactly, cut your brake line?" Jennifer asked.

Leigh Ann collapsed onto one of the dining chairs, covering her face with her hands. Sniping at each other, or contesting whose high school boyfriend deserved the "worst bet" label, wasn't helping a bit.

"Earlier you told me about the article in the *Atlanta Eye*," Jennifer reminded Leigh Ann.

Leigh Ann retrieved a newspaper from the counter and tossed it across the table.

Jennifer winced at the photo of Sheena and Mary Jo and skipped that article. She already knew what Teague had to say about Danny's murder. She didn't care to read what else he made up. She scanned through the write-up about Gavin that lay directly below. Out loud she read:

" 'Gavin Lawless, rising music star, told this reporter that repressed memories recently resurfaced during sessions with a prominent California regression therapist. Those memories became the basis for "Don't Forget," a ballad that is sure to rock the world of folk music as well as the city of Macon, where Jimmy Mitchell disappeared a number of years ago.

" 'Lawless, who may have witnessed his cousin's murder, suffered a breakdown following the incident. He's hoping additional sessions will fill in the story gaps and eventually lead to the prosecution of those responsible.' "

All Jennifer could do was shake her head. "So what do we do now? I don't feel good about your staying by yourself." Or with Gavin.

"Me, neither," Leigh Ann confessed.

"Want to crash at my place?" Jennifer offered.

"No offense, Jennifer, but a couple of ten-year-olds with slingshots could pretty much take us."

"Teri, then? She does have a brown belt in karate."

"You're joking, aren't you?"

"Monique? Her husband is a gun collector."

"Antique?" Sam asked.

Jennifer shook her head. "More like AK-47s. Uzis. You know, if someone makes it and it can run through twenty rounds in twenty seconds, he has at least one. Plus about three kinds of ammunition to use in it. The man could be his own gun show."

"Sold," Leigh Ann declared. "Do you think she'd mind?"

As crusty as she could sometimes be, Jennifer knew that Monique would do anything to help anyone in their writers' group. The question was whether or not Leigh Ann could put up with staying there.

"I'll give her a call," Jennifer volunteered, rising and taking up the receiver of the wall phone.

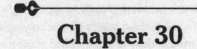

Chapter 30

As far as Jennifer was concerned, the gloves were off. It was time to take matters into her own hands. No more Mr. Nice Guy. She knew who won the "worst bet" boyfriend award, hands down. Besides, she could forget about getting any sleep that night.

When she'd handed the phone to Leigh Ann, Monique had given her express instructions to bring her work on a computer disk, so she could spend the time at her house writing, and to plan to call in sick at work. She didn't intend to let her out of her sight, not for one minute. She'd added that Leigh Ann needn't worry; her husband had shown her how to use at least half a dozen of his favorite weapons, evoking an image that Jennifer tried hard not to think about: Monique wearing a sweatband around her forehead, a shirt with the sleeves torn out, and crisscrossed leather bands of ammunition.

Her knuckles went white as she gripped the steering wheel of her little Beetle, angry that she had been put in this situation, angry that her friend was in danger, angry that Danny was dead.

It was late, and she knew she shouldn't be out by herself. But now that Leigh Ann was safely tucked away at Monique's—Sam had insisted on following them over to the Duprees and then had left as soon as they pulled into the driveway—she had one more stop to make.

Leigh Ann was a lousy liar. Her voice had a tendency to get the tiniest bit higher whenever she deviated from the truth. Jennifer knew her well enough to spot it right away. Of course, Gavin had told her where he was staying even if Leigh Ann had tried to deny it. Jennifer had made her crack during the car ride over to Monique's.

He'd gone all the way north to Forsyth, to the Holiday Inn. Not that far really, but out of the range that most people would be looking if they were scouring Macon for one Gavin Lawless. Macon had enough motels to keep someone busy for quite some time.

She parked the car in front of Room 117 and got out. It was close to two o'clock in the morning, but what the heck. Musicians kept late hours, or so she'd heard. Frankly, she didn't care if she woke him. He'd more than inconvenienced her with his reappearance in Macon, and he was going to answer for that inconvenience right now.

She could see just a hint of light through the break in the drapes. He must still be up, either that or he slept with the lights on. She'd been doing a lot of that herself lately. She pounded on the door with her fist.

After several seconds Gavin opened the door, a towel wrapped around his right hand. Without a word, he motioned her inside, locking the door behind her. Then he unwrapped the towel and lay the gun that had been hidden beneath it next to the lamp on the bedside table.

She noticed a bad scrape across his forehead and a bandage wrapped around most of his forearm.

"They're coming after Leigh Ann," Jennifer said, anger seething in her chest.

Gavin cocked his head, and for a moment Jennifer

thought she saw what looked like panic ripple beneath his features. "Is she all right?"

She nodded, swallowing hard. She felt somehow used by *them*, whoever they were, as though she were now their instrument, their vocalization of the threat to stop whatever it was that he was doing. "Her brake line was cut, but she couldn't have made it anywhere. Too many stops and starts in that parking lot."

"Good. So where is she?"

"Someplace safe. I'm sure she'll call you tomorrow even though I told her not to."

Gavin raised his chin and offered her a grudging grin. "I'm beginning to understand why Leigh Ann likes you."

"I wish I could say the same about you. You must be crazy to give a story like that to Teague McAfee."

That made his grin slip away, and she was almost sorry she'd said it. He seemed very alone somehow, hiding out in that motel room with no one to watch his back while he slept. She hadn't seen him speak to anyone else the night of the reunion.

"I know what you're doing, Gavin," she told him. "You need to stop it. This is serious. People are getting hurt."

"I can't stop it, woman. I didn't start it." He shook out a cigarette from a pack lying next to the gun, his hands trembling, and lit it with a match, sucking the smoke deep into his lungs. Then he lay down on the bed, one arm folded behind his head against the pillow, his legs crossed at the ankles and his boots propped on the bedspread. The sheets lay crumpled beneath him. Maybe she had awakened him.

She pulled out the straight-backed chair from the desk and sat down stiffly. His seeming relaxation was a kind of power ploy, her discomfort her response.

"How do you know that Jimmy Mitchell is dead?" she asked.

He raised an eyebrow at her.

"I don't necessarily believe you killed him, if that's what you're thinking. I don't think you would have come back and stirred things up this way if you had." At least she hoped he wouldn't. She'd prefer to think of that gun whose barrel was pointing straight at her on the table as a defensive weapon. "Repressed memories won't hold up in a court of law."

He drew hard on his cigarette and blew smoke in her direction. "So?"

"You've got to tell somebody everything you remember sooner or later. The fewer people who know, the more danger you're in."

That observation didn't cut it. He was studying her, obviously unconvinced that she cared one whit about his being in danger. "Give me one good reason I should tell you anything."

"My gut tells me that whatever happened to Jimmy Mitchell all those years ago is the reason Danny Buckner was murdered. Danny was my friend. Now Leigh Ann has been threatened. What's going on is personal to you. What's going on is personal to me, too."

Gavin rose up on the bed, pulling his legs up Indian style. He must have some pretty strong abs under that dingy T-shirt. He leaned forward, his elbows resting at his knees, and took another puff on his cigarette. He coughed, and said, "Okay."

She held her breath and leaned forward, too, as though somehow meeting him, at least symbolically, halfway.

"Jimmy told me he was going to see someone that night."

"The night of the prom."

"Right."

"Do you know who?"

He shook his head. "If I knew who, we wouldn't have to

go through all this bull. . . . I smoked a lot of weed back then. Getting high was one of the few things I did well. Sometimes I drank, too."

Jennifer noted the use of the past tense. "Were you high that night?"

"Feeling no pain." He flicked ashes into the ashtray he picked up off the bedside table.

"So how, exactly, do you know Jimmy's dead?"

He paused and stared at her for several seconds before saying, "I buried his body."

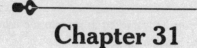

Chapter 31

Jennifer's jaw hung open as she stared at Gavin. "You buried him?"

Gavin nodded. "As best I can tell. Like I said, I was high when it happened." He ran a hand through his hair, the one with the cigarette.

She clamped her hands over her mouth to keep the words from coming out, to keep from telling him what a fool he'd been to do drugs, to let something fog his mind on a night when he needed to know exactly what was going on.

"First, let's go through what you actually remember, on your own," she said, consciously keeping the anger from her voice. "Jimmy called you that night and told you . . ."

"I'd seen him earlier in the day. In person. He said he was going out and not to come over trying to find him. He gave his parents some cover story about going to the movies with Ben Underwood. He said he'd found something out that he had to take care of."

"What do you mean, take care of? Was he planning to hurt someone?"

Gavin pursed his lips at her.

"I'm a very literal person," she explained. "I don't want to misunderstand what you mean."

"I guess he meant to warn whoever it was. Jimmy wasn't a fighter."

"How did you know where to find him?"

Gavin lifted himself off the bed and began to pace, as if the agitation of that night were stirring inside him. "He told me he was going down to the school. He said he'd have Ben bring him home, that he'd call when he got there. If he wasn't home by one, I was to come after him."

"So he knew he was in danger."

"No, Jesus, woman, follow what I'm saying. If he had, he would never have gone."

Gavin had adopted a most irritatingly condescending tone. But she didn't call him on it. She didn't want to take the chance he'd stop talking.

"He said he needed someplace private to talk. He said he planned to go down to the river, just below the high school."

"So you followed him down there, all alone, at one o'clock in the morning." Man, was he stupid.

"I know I headed over to the school sometime close to eleven."

"Because?"

"Because I didn't like the feel of it. And because I wanted to tell him that trying to reason with people who make a habit of screwing everybody over ain't gonna get you nowhere. If he had something on somebody, he should have gone to the police."

"Maybe he didn't have any evidence."

He gave her a superior smirk. "So what?"

"You were high when you went after him."

"Absolutely. I'd downed probably a six-pack. I don't know how much weed I had."

"And?"

"And the next thing I really remember is waking up in a hospital. They say a policeman found me walking along I-75 about four o'clock that morning. They said my clothes were all torn up. I don't remember any of that."

"When did you find this regression therapist?"

"About a year ago. I was finally making enough money."

"He helped you?"

"She. Yeah."

"So tell me, what did she help you remember?"

"I did go down to the river. I couldn't find Jimmy, so I worked my way down the bank."

"With a flashlight?"

"With the full moon. But yeah, I'm sure I had a flashlight."

She nodded, feeling the shivers take her once again. "And you found him."

His pacing stopped and he sank back down on the edge of the bed. "I found his body not all that far from the trees where I'd come out the first time. I'd missed him. He was lying in the shadows. I was looking for . . . something different." He paused, and she waited while he stubbed out the cigarette. "I remember the moisture on my hands when I touched him. He must have been soaked with water. He was so still. His skin had already started to cool."

"How could you be sure he was dead?"

"His eyes were wide open. They didn't move."

"You must have held your flashlight on him."

He nodded, lighting up another smoke. "After ten minutes without oxygen, they say the brain is irrevocably damaged. I figure it took me longer than that to find him. Have you ever seen a dead person?"

Once, up close and personal, she'd stared into a dead woman's eyes and fainted. Death, despite how people like to picture it as sleep, is something quite different. She'd seen it, and she was certain so had Gavin.

Gavin's experience, whatever it really was, had settled so deep inside of him that he'd pushed away the memories. Between the words, she heard his anguish. He had found

Jimmy, limp and dead, abandoned on the bank of the river. His friend, his cousin. Alone in the dark. She couldn't even imagine his horror. If it had been her, she probably would never have slept again.

"Why did you bury him?"

"Because, somehow, I knew they'd be back to get rid of him."

So the paranoia was nothing new. "They who?"

Again he shook his head, apparently exasperated with her.

"Okay, okay." She backed off. "Sorry."

"We—Jimmy and me—had a fight earlier that day. I . . ." He punched the pillow hard with his fist.

"That's why you had the regression therapy. You were afraid you might have killed him," she whispered.

He shook his head. "No way."

She could see the sweat bead on his forehead. She knew he was lying. It had to be his worst fear.

"Maybe he simply drowned," she offered.

"Swimming in the river at night? We weren't stupid enough to do that in the daytime. Besides, his neck was broken. When I lifted his head to try to give him mouth-to-mouth, I could tell."

He'd apparently forgotten to add that little bit of information earlier. In his dreams, at least, he'd tried to save him. "I see. So you buried him."

"Damned right. Before they could come back and dispose of Jimmy. I picked him up and carried him a good ways up the bank. I remember the weight on my back."

"How were you able to bury him? You couldn't have had any tools with you."

"I found some kind of overhang, and I shoved his body back up under it, just to get him safe, so I could have time to think. Then I realized how soft the dirt was. It had stormed the night before. I got on top and loosened the dirt from above using my pocketknife, the flashlight, and the weight of my body."

It couldn't have been much of a grave even then, probably just enough so no one would have noticed the body. Nobody, when they'd searched for Jimmy, had known to look along the river.

"Where exactly?"

"I'm not sure. The river seemed to dip back in that spot, and there was some kind of big tree right by there. The roots were what caused the overhang to form."

She nodded. Stupid kid, worrying about a killer coming back who probably had no intentions—

"I was patting mud into place when I heard them. At least I think I was. I remember dirt all over my hands."

He wasn't looking at her anymore, but at the far corner of the room. She didn't dare speak or make a sound for fear he'd stop.

"They had those large flashlights like in *E.T.* and the *X-Files*. The beams cut back and forth through the trees and the bushes, rising into the sky and sweeping back across the clear areas like a searchlight.

"I saw the lights before I saw the shadows. I felt like I was on some kind of bad acid trip, like some kind of homing device was shooting out. Looking for Jimmy. Looking for me.

"I couldn't move. I couldn't speak. I rolled back among the trees. I didn't have the courage to come out and confront them. Hell, I couldn't even breathe."

"How do you know they were after Jimmy?" she whispered.

"One of them said something like 'We're too far down. I left him back that way.' That's when the lights swung back around and seemed to go back in the direction they'd come in."

"You don't know who they were?"

He shook his head.

She felt so sorry for him that if he'd been almost anybody else, she'd have gone to him and put her arms around him. He didn't know what was real and what scenes he'd patched in from movies or TV or his favorite novels. Repressed memories were notoriously unreliable. Except the ones that weren't.

"How many people were there?"

"I don't know."

"All males?"

He shrugged. "The one who spoke had a deep voice."

"You never told anyone."

"I told you, I couldn't remember. It's coming back, though. The more I talk about it, the more real it seems."

"Ben Underwood took the blame."

Gavin looked straight into her eyes. "He was questioned, never accused."

"You might have cleared him." She didn't add, *and ended his nightmare.*

"How do you figure that? I don't know who killed Jimmy. I don't know who was out there that night. How do *you* know it wasn't Ben?"

Perhaps the guilt he carried for Underwood's suffering was why he'd come back. That and the fear that had settled deep into his bones.

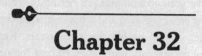

Chapter 32

She couldn't sleep much of what was left of that night. Gavin's words kept replaying in her mind. She had to know if what he told her was the truth. Was Jimmy really buried somewhere along the riverbank?

Gavin couldn't go down there; that was obvious. Who knew what would happen if he actually came face-to-face with his cousin's body? He'd fought for years for stability.

"I'm going to tell you something, Leigh Ann, but you can't tell Gavin. Understand?" She glanced at her watch. It was barely nine o'clock in the morning. She'd interrupted her friend's Grape-Nuts.

There was a pause on the other end of the line.

"You're going to have to decide who you trust here, Leigh Ann."

"Can't I trust you both?"

"I need to settle this once and for all. I need to know if Gavin has been telling the truth."

"He has," Leigh Ann insisted. "Whatever he told you, it's true."

How could she be so sure? Gavin wasn't.

"Promise me, Leigh Ann."

A loud groan came across the line. "All right, I promise."

Jennifer wished she could see her, wished she could check for crossed fingers and crossed toes. She had to tell somebody. She didn't dare go out there alone with nobody knowing where she was. Not that it had saved Jimmy Mitchell. But who could she tell? Sam would try to stop her, and Dee Dee would call Sam. Or the police.

Still, she had to know. Was Jimmy Mitchell really dead?

"I'm going out along the Ocmulgee tonight, after dark."

"Are you out of your mind? Why?" Leigh Ann sputtered. "Why would you—"

"To find Jimmy Mitchell's body."

There was another long pause on the other end of the line. "I always suspected you were crazy, Jennifer, but I loved you anyway. But now you've gone over the edge. You need professional help. You can't—"

"Gavin told me he buried Jimmy's body somewhere along the river, not too far from the high school. There's only one area that's accessible from the road, so it's got to be in that stretch."

"Buried his body? Are you nuts? Gavin didn't kill—"

"I'm not saying he did, and neither is he. Just trust me, Leigh Ann. If we can do this, we can settle what happened to Jimmy once and for all. Then maybe Gavin can find some peace."

"You talked to him? I told you where he was in confidence. How could you?"

"Don't worry about it. He wouldn't have told me if he didn't want someone to know."

"But why go at night? People in those creepy horror movies always wait until dark to go poking around. The ones who are hunting vampires—you'd think *they*, at least, would have the sense—"

"It's public property. I can't go digging on public property in the daylight. I'll get arrested, and I certainly don't want to have to explain to the police or anyone else what I'm up to."

"There are lots worse things than getting arrested," Leigh Ann reminded her. "What I do for you. Okay. What time do we go?"

"No, Leigh Ann. I'm going alone." Her protest was more for show than for anything else. She'd been hoping from the beginning that Leigh Ann would volunteer to come along. She just couldn't admit it, even to herself. She wasn't the bravest person in the world. Or the stupidest.

"Give me a time, Jennifer. I don't want to have to wait down there in the dark for you to show up."

"How's ten sound to you?"

"Late."

"I know, but the days are getting longer."

"Where do you propose we park?"

"There's no access to that area by car. I say we park at the high school and walk down through the woods."

"That's a long way."

"Got any better ideas?"

"Nope. I'll bring some flashlights."

"Good."

"Okay. See you then."

Leigh Ann hung up. Just like that. Leaving Jennifer committed to wandering the banks of the Ocmulgee. In the dark. Looking for a dead body.

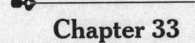

Chapter 33

Jennifer rolled her little Beetle into a parking space, cut the engine, and checked again to make sure the doors were locked. The parking lot of Riverside High School was deserted. She felt a shiver raise the hair on her arms, and wondered why coming to look for Jimmy's body had seemed like a much better idea in the daylight.

Muffy snorted and plopped her head between the bucket seats, resting her jaw on the parking brake. Jennifer was counting on the dog's instincts to alert them to danger, both of this earth and otherwise. So far Muffy only looked bored. That had to be a good sign.

Leigh Ann had better not be late. She wanted to get this over, before she had too much time to think about it.

She checked to make sure the ski mask was still snug in her pocket. She'd donned a black turtleneck and black jeans. She would put on the mask, if necessary, and would simply disappear in the dark. Or so she hoped. Okay, it was a ridiculous idea, but she'd brought it anyway. There certainly was no way to make Muffy disappear or even be quiet.

Lights flashed in the rearview mirror, and she heard the soft crunch of gravel on asphalt. She flipped her head around so she could see out the left side of the car. A white Lincoln slid up next to the Beetle. Leigh Ann? She knew she'd be driving a loaner from the garage, but hardly imagined it'd be a Town Car. A place Leigh Ann did business with would more likely supply a rent-a-wreck.

As she watched, all four doors burst open at once. Panic washed over her. She'd seen too many gangster movies. Heck, she'd seen too many movies, period.

She shoved Muffy into the backseat, turned the key in the ignition, prepared to stomp the gas pedal, and twisted her head to the back too rapidly. A sharp, cramping pain shot down her neck. It stopped her long enough to get a glimpse of the four figures, also dressed in black, rapidly surrounding her car.

There was something familiar about them. A curve here, a movement there. She could tell they were all female.

She switched off the motor and got out, almost shutting Muffy's nose in the door. "What the heck are all of you doing here?" she demanded angrily of Teri, Monique, and April in a whisper so loud she shouldn't have bothered. Leigh Ann crouched in the background.

"You can hardly expect us to allow you and Leigh Ann to go off on some ill-considered expedition on your own," Monique declared, leaning a pickax up against her knee and adjusting black leather gloves. "Grave robbing requires a certain expertise."

"I told you not to tell anyone," Jennifer barked at Leigh Ann, more than a little irritated. Then she suddenly wondered exactly what kind of grave-robbing experience Monique had.

"No, you told me not to tell Gavin," Leigh Ann said defensively, coming forward. "You know I'm staying with Monique. Exactly how did you expect me to slip out of her house at night without her knowing?"

"Safety in numbers," April declared. She was carrying an insulated bag about the size of a vanity case.

"What's with the luggage?" Jennifer asked.

"Provisions. Who knows how long it may take us to locate the remains?"

Jennifer could only shake her head and hope none of them brought a tent. She hoped to prove whether Gavin's memories were real—she was still holding hard to the Jimmy-in-Vegas scenario—not actually find "the remains."

Teri held flashlights in both hands, each one longer than her forearm. She hefted them in such a way that it was obvious they could serve as blunt instruments should the need arise. "We need to move out before the authorities get wind of what's going down," she said, handing one of the lights to Jennifer and adjusting the camp shovel slung over her shoulder.

She had to be dreaming, Jennifer told herself. Maybe she'd fallen asleep in the car waiting for Leigh Ann, and all of this was merely a nightmare. She'd envisioned a discreet search of the riverbank, not a weekend bivouac with Monique as commanding officer.

Muffy barked loudly from the car. Jennifer could see her nose pressed against the small back glass, her tail flipping back and forth in the shadow. She wasn't about to be left out.

"All right, ladies, I want us all back here in no less than two hours," Monique ordered, checking her watch. "Remember, no wandering off. Should you become separated from the group, blow one of these." She stuffed whistles attached to neck bands in each of their hands.

Part of Jennifer wanted to salute. Another part wanted to go AWOL.

"Jennifer, retrieve Muffy from your car," Monique ordered.

Grumbling under her breath and wondering how she could have so completely lost control, Jennifer went over to the Volkswagen, pulled the dog from the backseat, and clipped a leash to her collar.

April followed after her. "Leigh Ann seemed a little vague on the plan. All I heard was something about a dead body."

"Where are your babies?" Jennifer asked, not at all ready to address the idea of grave digging, and hoping against hope that April's children weren't waiting in car seats inside the Lincoln. She could only imagine them strapped, one on each of April's hips, as they trekked through the woods.

"Craig's got them. I left formula for Colette," April explained, spraying the hems of Jennifer's jeans with a healthy blast from an aerosol can.

"What's that?" Jennifer asked, dodging the spray as best she could while wrestling with Muffy.

"Tick spray. Can't go walking in the woods without it," April declared.

She was having a nightmare, all right, just not the sleeping kind.

Chapter 34

Down among the trees, away from the light of the parking lot, it was country dark. It would have been impossible to negotiate the fifteen-minute hike to the river without Teri's flashlight, although Muffy did a fair job of pulling her along. She only got her leash tangled around one tree.

Once out of the foliage and its treacherous roots covered by underbrush, they all switched off their lights. The moon, on the wane, still glowed enough so they could move about without stumbling over rocks or debris.

"We need to develop a systematic plan for searching the area," Monique told the group. Then she singled out Jennifer. "We haven't got all night. Which way, Jen? Up or down the river?"

"Up." She pointed north. "We're looking for a large tree with an overhang in front of it that's been broken away."

With her wet tongue, Muffy found Jennifer. Then Jennifer took the leash back from April, who had come up behind her and who promptly shoved a Power Bar into her hands. "To keep up your strength."

"No dice," Monique declared, slinging the pickax back over her shoulder.

"It looks like this should be the place," Jennifer insisted. "You can see where the bank used to jut out."

"And this water poplar is huge," Leigh Ann declared, patting its trunk, "just like you said Gavin described it. Its roots helped hold the dirt to form the overhang."

"Maybe so," Teri agreed, lying on her back in the crook of the bank just beneath the tree. She swept the area one more time with the beam of her flashlight. "But if something was ever concealed under here, it's long gone now." She pulled herself up and out, brushing off the back of her pants with her hands as she held the flashlight under her chin.

"Maybe this isn't the place. Maybe ours is further up," Leigh Ann offered.

"We've already been up as far as the bank will let you walk," April reminded her.

"But—" Jennifer began.

"We're moving out," Monique declared. "Police your area. I don't want any litter left on site."

No wonder Monique was so good at dialogue, Jennifer mused. She fell into character as though she were born to it.

"But—" Jennifer tried again.

Leigh Ann put an arm around her shoulder and tugged her along. "We'll get the answers, Jen. I promise. Just not tonight."

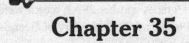

Chapter 35

"He almost had me," Jennifer admitted the next morning, pacing back and forth in front of Sam's desk at the *Telegraph* offices. "Gavin lied and I believed every word."

"So you didn't find a body. What he told you might still be true," Sam pointed out, reared back in his chair.

She stopped abruptly and leaned toward him, pinning him with her look. "That body didn't just walk away."

Sam leaned forward, too. "Probably not, assuming it was there at all. Twelve years is a long time, and there is wildlife in the area."

"True. But wouldn't someone have noticed if a dog or a raccoon or whatever the heck lives near the river had dug out some human bones?"

A colleague passed by, stopped to stare, then smiled and moved on when Sam nodded at her. "They think we're fighting."

"Well, they're wrong," she snapped, throwing herself into a straight-backed chair. "Now we're right back where we were. We still don't know if Jimmy Mitchell is dead."

"His folks think he is."

She stared at him. "You talked to them?" If so, he had more courage than she did.

He nodded. "They're a close family. His mother insists that even if he didn't contact them for whatever reason, he would have gotten in touch with Gavin or Ben. He wouldn't have let Ben be persecuted the way he was."

"Unless—"

"No unless if he were alive. Jimmy had his whole future planned out. His grades and his PSAT scores were excellent. He wanted to attend the University of Georgia for an undergrad degree in political science, then on to law school and eventually wind up a judge."

"His cousin drank and smoked pot."

"And he didn't." Sam shrugged.

"But he ran away several times."

"Not far and only to stay with friends. He always called to let his parents know where he was."

"What did Jimmy's parents have to say about Gavin? I'm sure you asked."

"He's basically a good kid. Doesn't handle pressure well."

"No kidding." She was getting sarcastic, and she knew Sam didn't deserve it. "Look, I'm sorry. Seems I've been saying that to you a lot lately. I appreciate what you've done."

"No problem. Tell you what. I'll speak to one of the local wildlife enthusiasts. Maybe he can suggest some other place along the river that might match Gavin's description. He could have been confused."

"Good," she said, pulling the straps of her purse up onto her shoulder, "but we searched every inch of that bank that's accessible from the path down from the school."

"You leaving?" he asked.

"Yeah. I've got another question I need answered."

"What's that?"

"Why Jimmy was meeting someone that night."

* * *

"Monique's not happy about you stopping by and taking me for lunch and not asking her along," Leigh Ann told Jennifer as she unwrapped her chicken sandwich.

"I know. I saw her face. I promise to make it up to her, but I need to talk to you alone." Jennifer pulled out a napkin just in time to catch the mayonnaise that was about to drip onto the tabletop.

"You really ought to try one of these," Leigh Ann gushed. "They are so good. Oh, sorry. I forgot. You can't. It's just that you look so pitiful with only your salad."

Didn't matter. She wasn't hungry anyway. Lunch was only an excuse to get Leigh Ann out. All she wanted was a cold drink and some answers. Fast food places didn't cater to non-meat eaters.

"Leigh Ann, you knew Jimmy."

"Sure." She took another big bite of sandwich.

"Did you know he and Candy were friends?"

"Yeah, now that you mention it, but she kept that relationship on the QT. Why he wanted to hang with her, I have no idea."

"You're kidding. Candy was adorable."

Leigh Ann rolled her eyes. "She was one of the biggest bitches—"

"No way. She's so polite—"

"Maybe now and maybe before. But when Jimmy was with her, no way would I go near them. She'd bite your head off if you looked at her funny. That is, when she wasn't crying."

"She was having trouble with Al."

"That jock she married?" Leigh Ann shook her head. "He was a real . . . fill in your favorite insult. But he worshiped her. He didn't mind screwing over everybody else, but not Candy. He treated her like gold. He wanted her back really bad."

"So why'd they break up?"

"The usual teenage I'm-too-young-to-be-so-committed-I-need-to-date-other-people routine. As if love were valid only between certain ages of life. People should have figured this out by now. The greatest love story of all time was between two fourteen-year-olds."

"Romeo and Juliet. That ended badly," Jennifer pointed out, poking at her salad. It was wilted and totally unappetizing.

"No lie. You'd think old Will could have lightened up just a bit, cut the kids a break."

"So if it was Candy's idea to give the relationship a rest, why was she so sullen?"

"Beats me. She had the biggest man at school knocking on her door. You'd think that might ease her mood."

"Who?"

"Seth Yarborough. But then he dropped her flat after the second date."

"How do you know that?"

"They didn't date again. I can't imagine her, or anyone else, turning that hunk down. That was about the time she got really bad. Gavin told me Jimmy was afraid she might kill herself."

"Candy." Jennifer knocked again and called through the closed door. "I only need a minute of your time. Please."

The door opened a crack and Candy peered over the security chain.

"Can I come in?"

"I'd rather you didn't."

"I need to know about Jimmy, who he was going to meet the night he disappeared."

"I already told you I don't know."

"I believe you. His cousin Gavin told me Jimmy had

found out something, something he had to take care of. I think he was doing it for someone else."

Candy blanched, her pale complexion becoming a startling white. "Oh, God. Don't you understand I can't?"

"He told me Jimmy met someone down by the river, someone who killed him. Later, people came looking for his body."

She stared at Jennifer, truly frightened.

"Do you know where Al was that night? I think I know where Danny was."

"Go home, Jennifer, and count your blessings. Be thankful I warned you."

"Warned me—"

The door slammed shut in her face, and no amount of ringing the bell could get Candy to open it again.

Chapter 36

Sam's voice sounded distant over the phone line. "I got hold of that naturalist friend of mine."

"Yeah? So what did he say?" Jennifer asked, feeding Muffy the crumbs left over from her jelly toast breakfast. She hiked up the pants of her flannel pajamas. She hadn't been eating well since Danny died—the meal at the Casablanca excepted—and she could tell it in her waistline.

"He said if a body was buried in a shallow grave down on the riverbank twelve years ago, there's no way it would still be there."

"I don't see why not. Bodies lie buried for—"

"He told me about the flood."

The flood. She'd completely forgotten. Six years ago the Ocmulgee had jumped its banks and stopped Macon cold, leaving them without fresh water for weeks. Showers had become a fond memory, and business had virtually ceased. The president declared Macon a disaster area, and bottled water was trucked in from all over the country. It hadn't once occurred to her when she'd gone looking for Jimmy's body.

"That recent flood in the Carolinas was so bad," Sam said, "that it floated coffins out of the cemetery."

"That happened here, too. I think some of the bodies even slipped their coffins. Can you imagine? It must have looked like something out of *Poltergeist*. Dead bodies and coffins bobbing along the river like gruesome buoys." She held her breath. "What did they do with those bodies?"

"They reburied them."

"Do you think they might have had one left over?" she suggested.

She could hear his sigh over the line.

"It's not as far-fetched as it might sound at first," she rushed on. "I don't know how many floated out, but isn't it possible they had an extra, one more than they had coffins?"

"Jennifer, we have no reason to believe—"

"All right, then, indulge me just this once." She could imagine him cringing over the phone. She'd already had her share of "just this once" many times over. "Go back to the river with me. In the daylight. If we can't find any evidence that someone was buried there, I'll drop the whole matter. I'll never mention Jimmy Mitchell's name again."

"You expect me to believe that."

"Not really. But I do expect you to go with me."

"You know we aren't going to find anything."

"You don't know that." She felt like a petulant child.

"I think I can slip away for a short while this morning," he offered. "Not too much going on and I have been working overtime."

She smiled with relief.

"Where should we meet?" he asked.

"I don't know any other way to get there except through the woods from the high school."

"Fine. Let's make it eleven o'clock."

In the daylight there could be no doubt. Gavin, repressed memory or not, had described the location perfectly. There wasn't another area quite like it anywhere on that particular section of the riverbank.

"So he knew this stretch of the river," Sam told her. "That overhang most likely was taken away by high waters. I don't see anything to indicate a body was ever buried here." The bright sunlight dappled his face through the leaves. It was truly a beautiful day. Too bad her mood didn't match it.

"Doesn't mean there wasn't one," she added. He looked at her but didn't say anything. He didn't have to. They both knew how stubborn she was. Once she'd bought into Gavin's story, it would take a lot for her to give it up.

Sam picked up a stick and flung it out over the water. It arced and then plopped on the surface, bobbing briefly and then rising to float with the gentle current.

"Are you satisfied yet?" he asked.

She sat down in the dirt with her knees bent, next to what was left of the overhang, symbolically answering his question. She sank back against the slope. Sometimes life could be unfair.

She picked up a pebble and tossed it toward the water. It landed at the river's edge. She could see it sitting there, refusing to go with the flow.

"I need to be getting back," he told her, "but I might could manage to make time for lunch if you think—"

She didn't hear the rest of his sentence. She leaned over and grabbed a handful of grass at the edge of the overhang. Vegetation had flourished so well in the last six years that grass, weeds, and everything green covered any scars left by the floodwaters. She was frustrated beyond belief. She ripped out the grass and tossed it into the air, watching it float down over her, making a mess.

"Does that make you feel better?" he asked.

"Yes, I think it does," she declared, her jaw firmly jutted out.

"Then go for it," he suggested.

She grabbed another handful, ripped it from the ground, and threw it upward, too. Then a third. When she reached for a fourth, she stopped.

Sunlight glinted off what looked like a funny-shaped pebble, long and thin, tangled in the exposed roots. She reached for it, bringing it close to her eyes.

"Oh, God." The words burst from her. Her fingers spread wide and the object fell from her hand onto her thigh. "Get it off me," she shouted, scrambling to her feet as though covered by a swarm of fire ants. She fled to Sam, wrapping her arms around him and burying her face against his chest. It couldn't be what she thought it was. It couldn't.

"What the heck? Did something bite you?" Sam said, wrapping her closer to him, patting her hair.

"Look at it," she ordered. "Look at that . . . that thing!"

He tried to pull back, but she wouldn't let him move. "I will if you'll let go of me."

Reluctantly, she loosened her grip. When she managed to force herself to turn in his direction, Sam was intent on an object he was rolling back and forth in his palm.

He looked up at her. She'd seen that look before and she didn't like it.

"I think you're right. I think someone was buried here."

She closed her eyes, Sam's words filtering like a swirl into her mind.

"Looks like you found one of his finger bones."

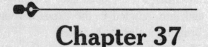

Chapter 37

The police were all over the place, their guns and night-sticks creaking in leather as they moved. She wished Sam hadn't called them, but he was right. They didn't have a choice.

One tall fellow cornered her and led off with a barrage of questions. She tap-danced around them as best she could, hoping beyond hope he'd never get to *why* they were at the river. If he did, how, exactly, could she avoid mentioning Gavin Lawless?

"I think I need to talk to a lawyer," Jennifer stated firmly.

"Miss, I don't see how that could possibly be necessary," the frustrated patrolman told her. "As I see it, you were simply down by the river enjoying the water with your boyfriend when you found an object that looked suspiciously like a bone."

"That sounds good. Put that down," Jennifer agreed, tapping the paper attached to a clipboard on which he was taking notes.

"We haven't even determined if the bone is human or animal. Probably something some dog drug down here and dropped."

Hadn't he ever seen a human skeleton? He was supposed to know what a finger bone looked like. She knew, and she'd only seen one in books.

"Once I write down the exact location—"

"Here," she insisted, pointing at the tangled tree roots jutting from what was left of the overhang. "That's where I found it. Can I go now?"

The policeman nodded. "Sign this report, and you're on your way."

She scanned his scribbles. They looked fine to her and incredibly innocuous. If she'd been writing it, the word "murder" would have been capitalized and underlined at least three times right next to the findings, which would have read "partial corpse."

"Thank you, officer." She smiled and handed back his pen and paper. Now if Sam had managed to keep his tongue . . .

"Those bodies," she said, once they were well into the woods and out of hearing distance from the police, "the ones that floated away during the flood. We need to find out what happened to any that weren't identified. Do you think one of them might be missing a finger bone? Maybe one with a broken neck."

"I'll go down to the coroner's office and ask, but on one condition," Sam told her. "I don't want you poking around trying to solve what you think is a murder case. We pay people to do that. They're called policemen."

"Right. Could you do it casually? It's only one simple question. I don't want to start something that's going to require a lot of explanation any more than you do. I don't agree with what Gavin's trying to do, but I don't feel I have the right to step in the middle of it. I'm afraid if he isn't more careful, he's going to get himself killed."

They ran into Seth Yarborough about five minutes farther up the path.

"Jennifer?" he said, his eyes darting back and forth from

Sam to her. "What are you doing here? Surely you're not the one who called in this report."

She nodded. "Technically, that would be Sam here."

"Are you talking with the press?" He cocked his head at Sam. "I thought I saw the two of you together at the reunion but . . ."

"Oh, you mean . . ." Seth wouldn't know about their relationship. "Sam was with me when we found . . ."

"You found what exactly?"

Jennifer and Sam exchanged looks.

"Well, I don't know. I thought it was a bone, maybe from some animal." She listened to herself talking as though viewing someone else. Why was she so stiff, so distant? The man had been kind enough to take her to lunch earlier that week. But he was one of *them*, one of the police, one of the people to be careful around.

She could feel Sam studying her face.

"The officers at the river have our statements," she assured Seth. "There wasn't anything to tell, but Sam thought we'd better report it anyway."

"That area's posted."

She frowned. "Are you going to give us a ticket?"

"Don't be silly. It's just not a good place to go. Kids go down there from school and get themselves in trouble."

"Right."

"If you've got any concerns, you come to me," Seth told her. "You don't have to call the police."

"I'll remember that," she promised.

He touched her hand and then shook Sam's. "It's nice seeing you both again."

He brushed past them, and she watched as he headed down toward the river.

Chapter 38

"Okay," Jennifer muttered to herself. Sam had dropped her off at home and then gone on to work. She was alone in her apartment, alone, except for Muffy and her thoughts.

"Let's say Jimmy was buried on that riverbank, and every word Gavin told me was true," she told Muffy. "And that Al got Danny and went down to the river looking for Jimmy's body that night. Why? Why would they do a thing like that?"

She paced the length of her living room. "What were you planning to do, Danny? Get rid of the body? You were on a date with me, for goodness sakes! The prom. What were you thinking?"

She wished she could shake him, make him tell her what had happened. "Something's come back up," she said aloud to herself. "Something I thought was long over and done." He'd wanted to talk to her about it. Why?

Jennifer sank onto the sofa, folding her arms. He knew. Of course, he knew. He knew who killed Jimmy. He had to if he was one of the ones who had gone to find the body. Only there wasn't a body, and he'd been left with the knowledge that someone had confessed to a murder that, in his mind, may or may not have happened. He couldn't go to the police. There wasn't any evidence of a crime. He never got the opportunity to make the choice: help cover up the crime or turn the murderer into the police.

So why did he want to talk to her? Because she knew he wasn't the murderer. Because she could testify that Al had come to the car and taken him away—after the murder had already taken place. But why his need for a private eye? That meant the murderer was still around and still dangerous. Danny was looking for more proof.

She sat back up and grabbed Muffy, who'd been pacing in front of her. "Don't you see," she told the dog, rubbing hard behind her ears. "Danny made that appointment with a lawyer, not to start divorce proceedings against Sheena, but to get some advice. He was preparing to go to the authorities because Gavin's song made it clear what he suspected: Jimmy was dead."

She looked deep into Muffy's eyes and asked, "Why? Why was Jimmy killed?"

Damn. Without that, none of it made sense.

The dog whimpered and Jennifer let her go.

She looked around the floor. Where, exactly, had those yearbooks Sheena left gotten to? They'd been next to the couch. She crouched down, Muffy jumping on the back of her legs, and ran a hand along the carpet. Near the skirt of the sofa she felt something hard. That's right. She'd shoved them under when Muffy decided they made a perfect perch.

She pulled them out and took the top one off the stack, opening it to the inside cover. Sheena had filled all of the first page, printing her name in huge letters. Then she'd taken a pack of pens and alternated sentences, following all the colors of the rainbow in order.

Jennifer scanned the almost illegible, angular scrawl. Suggestive fluff. About what she would expect. No reference to Jimmy or prom or much of anything else.

Most of the other entries in the front were typical. Keep

in touch. Call me over the summer. Have a great time in college. Etc., etc.

Jennifer hadn't signed it. What would she have to say even if they'd been talking?

She flipped on through to the advertising section in the back. On a page where an office supply store and a dry cleaners wished the graduating class every future success, there were entries from Mick, then Al, and finally Candy.

Hey, hey, hey, Bro. We actually made it all the way to graduation. Too cool for words, man. Two and a half more months and I'm outta here for good. I ain't never coming back. Keep the faith. Mick.

A skull with a dagger dripping blood was drawn in pen next to his name. He was good, Jennifer had to admit, if a little dramatic with his subject matter. And a bit premature with his plans to escape Macon.

Danny, boy, we made it! Four years and all is cool, man. We rule!!! Keep your head, keep your tongue, keep your freedom. What's gone is gone and none of our business. The future shall be ours, my friend. Al.

A sweat broke out across her neck and forehead as her gaze found the final entry on the page.

In big round letters with little *o*s dotting the *i*s, Candy had written: *Danny. Next year's got to be better than this one. I wish you love. Candy.*

She'd seen that handwriting before. Candy told her she had warned her, but she didn't say when. The note had been slipped into her locker *after* Jennifer's breakup with Danny. The weight gain, the mood swings, the depression. The warning. It all made sense.

Oh, God. There it was, the final piece that made it all fit. She knew who Jimmy had met that night, who had killed him, and she even knew why.

She dove for the phone, punching in numbers as fast as

she could, Muffy tangling herself in the cord. Jennifer shoved her out of the way.

Sheena picked up on the second ring. "Yes."

"Go over to Candy's house. Take her and the kids someplace safe."

"Jennifer? What the hell are you—"

"Just do it, Sheena. Now."

She cut the connection and dialed again. She had more phone calls to make.

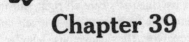

Chapter 39

"Seth, please, I need your help." Jennifer's throat was so constricted she could barely make the words clear over the phone line. "The real reason I was down at the river was because Gavin Lawless told me he buried Jimmy Mitchell's body there the night of our prom. I'm sure that bone we found is Jimmy's. The flood must have washed the rest of what was left of the body away."

"Calm down and tell me exactly what's going on. Are you saying Gavin Lawless confessed to Mitchell's murder?"

"No. I know all about the repressed memories he's been able to pull back up—surely you read the article in the *Atlanta Eye*—but there's more. He told me three people came back looking for the body to dispose of it that night." If she was wrong, she'd soon know.

"You've been talking to Lawless? Do you know where he is?"

"Not right now, but I can find out."

"Good. Where's your friend Leigh Ann?"

"Staying with a girlfriend."

"At least she's safe. I think you've jumped to some conclusions, Jennifer. I want you to take three deep breaths, settle down, and listen to me closely. I don't want to alarm you, but I did some checking on this Gavin Lawless. All that hoopla he fed to the *Eye* was a publicity stunt to promote his new song. He was never a patient of any regression therapist in California."

"You mean he's never been in therapy?"

"He's under a psychiatrist's care all right, but for paranoid schizophrenia. We've been trying to track him since the night of the reunion. He's dangerous, Jennifer. We've got to stop him. If we don't, he will kill again."

She forced herself to wait, counting away ten seconds very slowly. Finally, she said, "What do you want me to do? Get an address from Leigh Ann?"

"Yes, but don't let her know why you need it. Do we understand each other?"

"I'm sure we do. Seth, there's one more thing."

"What?"

"I think Gavin may be telling the truth. I remember."

There was a long pause on the other end of the line.

"What is it you remember?" he asked.

"Don't you see? That's why Danny wanted to talk to me the night of the reunion. He was going to the police to tell them everything he knew about what happened to Jimmy Mitchell. But he needed me to say I was with him when the murder took place, so he wouldn't be suspected. He couldn't risk the murderer trying to put it all off on him."

"Lawless has been pretty good at casting suspicion elsewhere."

"I didn't think anything of it at the time, of course, but it made me angry when Al came and took Danny away the night of the prom." She was grateful she was doing this over the phone. Seth couldn't see her hands shake as she lied. "I got out of the car and I followed them. I saw the person they met, the one that took them down to the river to look for the body."

"Are you sure?"

"Without a doubt."

"Are you going to the police?"

"I don't know yet. I was hoping you could help me decide. I need to weigh my options."

"Does anybody else know about this?"

"Nobody."

"All right. What if I pick you up about eight and we go someplace for cocktails?"

"Eight will be fine, but don't pick me up. I'll meet you at that new club, Casablanca."

"All right. I'll see you then."

She hung up the phone and looked at her watch. She only had four hours.

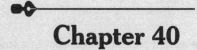

Chapter 40

The bar was already smoky when Jennifer arrived twenty minutes late. She spied Seth at a small table near the back, a glass of what appeared to be scotch on the rocks in his hand. He stood as she approached. She'd opted for a long, flowing, divided skirt and a scooped-neck, sleeveless top out of the same material. She carried a small beaded purse.

Seth took both her hands and leaned forward to kiss her cheek. "Let me get you something to drink." He beckoned a waiter who immediately came over.

"I'll have what he's having," Jennifer said confidently, pointing at Seth's drink.

"Nonsense. Bring the lady a Moroccan Fantasy."

Jennifer's face flushed. "I think I know what I want."

"You'll love it. It's a house specialty full of exotic juices. Very flavorful. You can't come here and not try it."

So much for Plan A.

"Come on," he told her. "We'll dance while he makes that up for you."

He took her hand in an unyielding grip and pulled her onto the dance floor, where he drew her to him. His mouth was at her ear. "So tell me, what did you see prom night?"

"I . . . I followed Danny and Al. I thought they might be meeting Sheena. Only, they weren't. They were meeting you."

She could feel his jaw muscles tighten against her cheek. "Gavin remembers three people coming down to the river to find Jimmy's body, but he doesn't know who they were."

"You think I was one of them."

She nodded her head.

"I had no reason to hurt Mitchell."

The music was so loud, she couldn't have pulled back to talk to him, even if he'd let her. He was crushing the very breath out of her.

"Candy told him about the date rape," she said. "She had to tell someone, and she was afraid of what Al might do if he found out. She never once thought that Jimmy might have the courage to confront you himself."

"Did Candy tell you this?"

"No. She's too frightened. But she did warn me not to date you when you asked me out in high school. She left a note in my locker. I thought it was from Sheena, but when I went through the yearbook and I saw her handwriting, I knew."

"Al didn't like it that Jimmy was messin' with his girl. Could be he decided to eliminate the competition."

"Perhaps, but Al's dead, Seth, and his murder can't be passed off as suicide even if Danny's can. They'll identify his body eventually. You took care of fingerprints and dental records, but they'll figure it out."

He loosened his grip enough that she could breathe. She pulled back and looked at his face. If there was a soul behind those eyes, she certainly couldn't see it.

"How would you know that?"

She shrugged. "I've got friends in the press."

"What do you want? Money?"

"Maybe."

"Let's go back and have our drinks."

He led her to the table, not letting go of her hand until he pulled out her chair and then pushed her down into it. A large round glass filled with blue liquid sat at her place. She lay her purse next to it.

"Try it," he insisted, taking his own seat.

She took a sip. It was sweet and fruity with lots of flavors vying for attention. "It's good."

"I knew you'd like it."

Seth reached for her hand and brushed the purse off the table. She bent to pick it up.

"I'm really sorry," he said. "I always liked you." He looked almost sincere, and on some level he probably was.

"Drink up," he told her. "This isn't the best place to conduct business."

"I kind of like it here. Plenty of people, plenty of noise." Too much noise, actually, for her purposes.

"I want a cherry for my drink," she announced.

"They don't come with one."

"Well, they should. Red would be so pretty in all that blue."

When Seth turned to raise his hand toward a waiter, Jennifer immediately dashed to the bar with her drink. But just as she reached it she stumbled and practically fell over a man in a wide-brimmed hat sitting on a stool.

"I am so sorry," she said, realizing that some of her drink had sloshed onto the man's shirt. Putting down her glass and grabbing a stack of napkins on the bar, she began to sponge off his damp shirt as best she could.

"It's not that wet, lady. No problem, really."

"Okay, but I'm really sorry," she said, putting down the napkins as Seth came up beside her.

Jennifer then turned to the bartender. "Put a cherry in there," she said, "and I want one of those little paper umbrellas, too."

"Give the lady what she wants," Seth told him.

The bartender added one of each, and Jennifer carried the drink back to the table.

"Are you satisfied?" Seth asked, as they settled back down.

"Totally."

"Good."

He drained his glass and ordered another one, while she slowly sipped hers.

"Do you have a figure in mind?" he asked.

"I was thinking maybe three-quarters of a million."

He shook his head at her. "You've got to be kidding."

"If I were kidding, I'd ask for a lot more. I think that's a reasonable figure for three murders. It breaks down to a quarter of a million apiece, not so much really. Certainly not when compared with what you'll make all those years you're not in prison."

He was studying her intently. She let her eyes flutter, then shook her head.

"Are you feeling all right?" he asked.

She shook her head as though to clear it. "A little woozy, maybe. My head feels like it's wrapped in batting. I must be coming down with something."

"Finish your drink and let's dance. It'll make you feel better."

She downed what was left of her Moroccan Fantasy and let him pull her onto the floor.

"Maybe if I eat something," she suggested, her words slurring.

"Sure. After we dance."

She slowed her steps and consciously willed her muscles to relax. Her eyes drifted shut again, and for a moment her head lolled backward. Suddenly, she shook her head and ran her hand over her face. "What's wrong with me?"

"I think you need some fresh air." He put his arm around her waist and pulled her toward the door. She turned back toward the bar and made an almost imperceptible shake of her head. Plan B was not her first choice.

Chapter 41

Outside, Seth scooped her up and carried her to his BMW. He opened the passenger side door and slid her into the seat, securing her seat belt. Making sure her skirt wouldn't catch in the door, he shut it. Quickly, she undid her purse and retrieved a slender cylinder that she clutched against her palm.

She shut her eyes as he opened the door and climbed in. "You *are* going to pay me my money, aren't you? You could consider yourself a supporter of the arts." She chuckled and then burrowed into the leather seat.

"Sure. Whatever you want."

As he backed out of the parking space, she yawned broadly and then excused herself. "Where are we going?" she asked.

"Not far."

He pulled out and headed up Zebulon Road. As soon as they crossed over the interstate, they'd be out of the developed area.

"Good. I don't want to go way off. You ruined my prom. You shouldn't have done that. My mama paid a lot of money for that dress. You ruined Sheena's reunion, too." Her words were more and more garbled. "Tell me why. Please, please, please, Seth. Tell me why?"

"You know why."

"Yes, but tell me. I want to hear you say it."

"Like you said earlier, Danny was going to the police. After he heard Lawless's song, he felt sure Mitchell was dead and that there had been a witness. He needed corroboration from you because I was an assistant district attorney and he was afraid of what I might do. He told Al, hoping Al would back him up. But Al told me. Unfortunately, Danny didn't see things our way. If he'd had any evidence, I suspect he would have turned me in back in high school. As it was, he could never be exactly sure what had happened down at the river between Mitchell and me."

"What about Al?"

"Al panicked when he saw Danny dead. He didn't buy suicide, so he and I had to have a talk. We went out in the woods and . . ."

She licked her lips and let her head drop farther down against the seat belt. "How'd you get the body to that abandoned house?"

"Wrapped it in a tarp and put it in the trunk."

"You didn't mean to kill Jimmy, did you, Seth? What did he threaten you with?"

"He said he'd see to it that charges were pressed."

"They couldn't have convicted you."

"No. But that wouldn't keep the colleges where I was accepted from withdrawing their offers of admission and scholarships."

Jennifer opened one eye and checked. No traffic. They were getting too far out. She sat bolt upright and sprayed pepper spray directly into Seth's face.

"You bitch," he choked, slapping the cylinder out of her hand. "What the hell do you think you're doing?"

His face had gone beet-red, his eyes swollen almost shut. Tears streamed down his cheeks as he gagged.

The car swerved and Jennifer grabbed the wheel. Somehow she managed to force her leg past the gear shift and into the driver's side of the floorboard between Seth's knees. She stomped on Seth's foot resting on the brake pedal. He howled just as she pulled the steering wheel hard to the right. They swerved off the road, stopping abruptly short of a large tree, first throwing them both forward, and then backward with so much force she was amazed the air bags didn't activate.

She struggled with her seat belt, but Seth, his face splotched, his eyelids puffed up like balloons, covered the latch with his fist. His other hand shoved a gun into the soft flesh of her throat. He didn't have to see to blow her head off. "What happened? I saw you drink it."

"I switched drinks with the guy at the bar." The gun dug further under her jaw. "You can't kill me here," she warned.

"Why not?"

"You'll get blood all over your car. You've committed three murders and left no evidence. Kill me now, and they'll have more than enough to convict you."

"What kind of game are you playing?"

"No game. We needed a confession and we got it."

He squinted at her, and she watched his gaze travel down her throat. Her top had shifted enough to reveal a tiny microphone clipped to her black bra.

"You're recording this?"

"Every word."

He let go of the seat belt and jerked the microphone loose, pulling the cord out with it and burning her skin. She released the seat belt as she felt the wire pop loose from the recorder taped to her leg. He snapped it out. "I ought to wrap this cord around your neck. . . . But like you said. Not here."

He threw the wire into the backseat and kicked open the driver's side door just as she managed to open her door latch. He swung back around and grabbed her right shoulder with his free arm and dragged her across into his seat, the gun back under her jaw and the gearshift badly scraping her ribs. "Just let me get you out of here."

She knew that once they were free of his car, he would kill her. He wouldn't wait to drag her into the trees. She only had this one chance. Both his hands were full. Both of hers were free.

She felt down through her pocket, the one she'd slashed open. The tape recorder containing Seth's confessions was strapped to her thigh. Her hand closed on an object taped just above it. She slipped it out of the leather and drew her hand back out.

All of the self-defense moves she'd ever been taught flitted through her mind, but Seth was too strong for her, and the car left no room to maneuver.

Her foot tangled in the seat belt as he tugged her farther across. It was never supposed to get this far. She had never planned to leave the parking lot of the restaurant. Where the heck were they?

Somehow she managed to twist sideways as he pulled her the rest of the way out of the car, her feet hitting the dirt. But she couldn't get her balance. She knew if she were going to stop him, she had to do it now. She twisted and rammed the gun barrel into his side, just above his waist, and fired.

Seth squealed and let loose, horrified as blood spilled over his shirt and trousers. Jennifer fell roughly to the ground.

"What do you think you're doing?" he demanded.

"I've got seven more shots," she told him, pulling the gun back up. "The next one will be further over, where something more vital is located."

Clutching his side with one hand, he pointed the gun directly at her head.

"Let it fall," a man's voice said. She hadn't had time to notice the green Saturn that pulled up behind the BMW. Ben Underwood stood, in full uniform, not six feet from them.

Seth jerked back. How much he could see out of those eyes was anybody's guess.

"You squeeze that trigger and you'll be dead before the bullet leaves the chamber," Ben told him.

Seth looked down at her with such hatred that, for a moment, she was afraid he'd kill her anyway. But, instead, he dropped the gun onto the ground.

Gavin Lawless kicked it away.

"Took you long enough," Jennifer grumbled.

"Got hung up at the light. What'd you expect us to do? Break the law?"

Chapter 42

"Jeez, Jennifer, I can't believe you actually shot Seth," Leigh Ann gushed. Then added, "With a gun."

"It's hard to shoot someone without one," Gavin pointed out as Jennifer shuffled them into her apartment. They had to leave for the airport in little over an hour.

"Did Johnny teach you to shoot like that?"

"It wasn't as if I could miss. The barrel was pressed against his skin." She shuddered. She couldn't bear to think about hurting someone, even someone who was about to kill her.

"Thanks for stopping by," she added.

"I was hoping you'd come to Jimmy's service," Gavin said.

"I would have, but I don't do funerals well. I turn into a blubbering mess and it becomes totally embarrassing for everybody involved. Besides, I'd like to hold onto that Jimmy-in-Vegas image."

"What?" Gavin looked confused.

"Nothing. Just Jennifer being Jennifer," Leigh Ann explained.

Dental records and a healed fractured femur confirmed that an unidentified skeleton that had surfaced during the flood and was later reburied was indeed what remained of Jimmy Mitchell.

"I take it your deal with Phoenix fell through," Jennifer said.

Gavin shook his head. His manner had changed. He seemed more relaxed, a little less haunted. "I'm just not ready to come back to Macon yet." His arm was tight around Leigh Ann's shoulders, as if he wasn't quite ready to leave either.

Tears glistened in Leigh Ann's eyes. She sniffed and then swatted at her cheeks, but her smile was firmly in place. "He's going back to California where he can work and still see his therapist."

Jennifer nodded. Life should be simple, but it never was. Gavin would leave and Leigh Ann would go back to writing her books, making happy endings for her characters while she waited for her own.

"Did you see the write-up Sam gave you in the *Telegraph*?"

"Yeah." Jennifer grinned. "How about that? Front page stuff. *'Mystery Writer Solves Triple Homicide.'* He even used my publicity photo."

"I think you ought to send copies of it when you submit your work to editors. Gives you more credibility."

Not a bad idea.

"How's the ankle?" Gavin asked.

"Not bad. The bruise on my side where Seth dragged me across the gearshift is giving me some trouble, but I'll be all right."

"You poor thing. I can't believe you took him on like that," Leigh Ann said.

"I didn't mean to."

"You weren't supposed to leave the club," Gavin reminded her.

"I know, but he wouldn't say anything that we could use against him. I was the only one talking. He just threw in some noncommittal comments every now and then. As it was, he could have used the tape against me, probably even charged me with blackmail if he'd known I had it—that is, if the words were intelligible. It was too noisy in there. I didn't really expect him to pick me up, throw me in the car, and take off out of the parking lot so fast. Where were you guys anyway?"

"Behind you as fast as we could get there, but we were parked on the other side of the lot. Everything happened a little fast."

"You weren't actually drugged, then," Leigh Ann said.

"Of course not. I knew what Seth had used on Danny and who knows how many women. My first plan was to switch drinks with him and get him to confess to me when he slipped into a relaxed, suggestible state. But the creep insisted on ordering for me. Of course, Plan B took that possibility into account. Gavin was watching from the bar so he could have the bartender fix him what I had, and I could make the switch with him. At least that part went well."

"Monique isn't pleased with you."

"She'll have to stand in line. Sam isn't speaking to me."

"You can't tell it by reading the newspaper."

"Furious but proud. It's a confusing combination. He'll be over in a few minutes, so he can *not* speak to me in person. Has Ben left? I was hoping to thank him one more time."

Gavin nodded. "He took off from the church. It was hard enough for him to take as much time off as he did. It took some fast talking on my part to convince him to come in the first place."

"You make for strange friends," she observed.

"Yeah, I guess we do." Gavin gave her a heartbreaker of a smile. So that's what had captured Leigh Ann.

"How's Candy?" he asked.

"Better. When Al didn't come home the night of the reunion, she had her suspicions. By the third day, she'd figured it out. She just didn't know what to do. She was terrified of Seth, and she had the children to think of. She knew he'd get around to her if she gave him the chance."

"Have you heard from Sheena?" Leigh Ann asked.

"Mick's keeping her busy, thank goodness." Both for her sake and for Jennifer's. "Can I get you two a soda or something?"

Leigh Ann shook her head. "We've got to be going."

Of course. They needed some time alone together. She walked them to the door and opened it. Leigh Ann hugged her, and Gavin leaned over and kissed her cheek.

"I might just have to write a song about you," he told her.

Now wouldn't that be a kick.

Suddenly, Muffy vaulted past them and down the hall toward the elevator. Sam was just getting off.

"We better go," Leigh Ann said, hugging Jennifer again, "so the two of you can *not* talk."

Sam shook Gavin's hand, hugged Leigh Ann, and walked right past Jennifer into her apartment as though he didn't see her. She shut the door after him.

"You're not supposed to associate with someone when you're not speaking to them," she told him. "You certainly shouldn't come to their home and make yourself comfortable."

His shoes were already off, along with his jacket. She watched as he pulled off his tie, rolled up his sleeves, and then propped his feet on the coffee table as he relaxed on the couch.

She sat down on the arm.

"Bring me a beer, woman."

"It speaks, and what funny words it says. You need to go back to Mattel and get reprogrammed."

He grabbed her and squeezed her to him.

"Watch the ribs," she gasped out.

He loosened his grip but refused to let go. "Promise me you'll never do anything that idiotic again."

"I certainly will try. What's the latest on Seth?"

"He's trying to get the confession thrown out on the basis that it was illegally obtained by the police."

"Is he nuts? I wasn't working for the police."

"Well, he's saying you were. But don't worry. I can't imagine he could be successful. We still have the drug found on his person and the attempted murder charge. He's claiming he was only trying to defend himself, that it was you who was trying to murder him. He won't get away with it, but Candy was right to be afraid of him."

"I should have shot that bastard again."

"Don't say that on the stand. It won't go well for our side."

"I have two witnesses," she offered.

"A mentally ill druggie—"

"He wouldn't dare."

"—and a former suspect who has a personal interest in someone else being convicted of Jimmy Mitchell's murder."

"A young and highly decorated Gulf War hero. Surely there's fiber evidence in Danny's car if nothing else," she insisted.

"Seth will say he was part of the investigating team. Unavoidable contamination."

"Damn. He is good, isn't he? How about the gun?"

"Not the same one that killed Al."

"It has to be somewhere. So does the tarp he wrapped Al's body with after he killed him."

A knock sounded. She went to the door and peered through the peephole. Teague McAfee. He and Sam mixed like oil and water. She opened the door a crack.

"What's up now?" she asked.

"There she is, our little hero. Aren't you going to invite me in?"

"Can't do it. I've got someone with me."

"Ah, yes, the lucky man in your life. Someday you'll be sorry you treat me so shabbily, Marsh."

"Right. I take it you went to the funeral."

"Wouldn't have missed it. That weasel Yarborough is trying to slip through the legal cracks."

"So it would seem."

"Not to worry. I'm about to seal them up. Too bad you don't have time for me to tell you about it."

"Spill it, Teague," she warned.

"I just wanted to let you know, I'll get the evidence you need."

"How do you plan to do that?"

"Creeps like Yarborough treat everybody like crap and think they can get away with it. I've got his two ex-wives and one soon-to-be who are all stepping up to the plate. I've never seen any three women more intent on screwing over one guy.

"The last wife supplied the locations of three safety deposit boxes. A bill for the most recent one, opened the Monday after the reunion, came to her house. The bank hadn't put through a change of address yet, and she opened the envelope, yeah right, by mistake. Should be interesting to see what's inside the boxes. The police are getting a warrant even as we speak. Catch my article in Wednesday's paper."

She pushed the door open, grabbed him and threw her arms around him. "Teague, sometimes I love you in spite of yourself."

"Hey, Marsh, remind me to save your ass more often."

She pulled back, remembering exactly who it was she was hugging.

Sam came up behind her at the door. "Have we got company?"

"Not really. Teague was on his way to write up his account of Jimmy's funeral."

"Right. Well, you kids have fun," Teague told them as Jennifer shut the door.

Her mother was right. Seth Yarborough had gotten around to treating everybody in his life badly, and he was about to pay for it. With that thought, maybe she could finally get some sleep for the first time in two weeks.

Epilogue

Jennifer stared at the white of the computer screen as black letters appeared almost as if by magic, her fingers flying across the keys.

These words stood by themselves, part of no book or short story. A promise, if only it were hers to make.

It'd been years since they'd seen each other. He was older, heavier, but somehow wiser as she searched his eyes. The passion was still there, the depth of feeling, the edge of uncertainty, but what most startled her was what wasn't there: the depth of sadness that had enveloped his soul and left its mark on his every thought, word, and deed.

Was it finally time? Had he at last put to rest all the demons of his past? He seemed to think so. That's why he'd called her, wasn't it? And written her. And sent her two dozen red roses. He was back, and this time he wasn't going anywhere.

She hugged him to her as if she'd never let him go. Never again. They would face whatever life threw at them head on. Together.

Jennifer pressed the Save button. This one was for Leigh Ann.

JUDY FITZWATER AND
JENNIFER MARSH

(Let me preface this interview by saying that I met with a certain amount of hostility when I approached Jennifer about talking with me. As professional as she is about her writing, she harbors some resentment for my playing Watson to her Sherlock. She insists that I'm not always accurate, especially in relating her inner feelings, and complains that I make her seem much more neurotic than she actually is. The fact that I'm published as a result of her adventures and she has yet to see any of her own writing in print remains a sticking point. However, two cappuccinos heavy with whipped cream helped her to warm up to the idea. Plus a promise to ask my editor to review some of her work.)

JUDY: **Jennifer, trouble seems to follow you around. How do the people close to you react to the number of dead bodies that you stumble upon?**

JENNIFER: For heaven's sake, Judy, it's not as if I actually go out looking for corpses. They just sort of find me. Although, I suppose, in the death of literary agent Penney Richmond (which you chronicled in *Dying to Get Published*), I was more of an active participant. Sam was pretty angry about how I got myself mixed up with that one.

JUDY: **Sam's that good-looking investigative newspaper reporter.**

JENNIFER: Right. He works for the *Macon Telegraph*. As I was saying, he wasn't so understanding, but my coworker Dee Dee (I help her with her catering business) and my whole writers' group—Teri, Leigh Ann, April, and Monique—were behind me all the way. So were Mrs. Walker, an elderly lady I met in Atlanta, and her friends. They knew I couldn't kill that despicable creature Penney, just as I knew Mrs. Walker couldn't have killed her slimy ex-husband Edgar.

JUDY: **I remember. I wrote about Mrs. Walker's troubles in *Dying to Get Even*.**

JENNIFER: And then, of course, there's the Diane Robbins case in which I teamed up with private detective Johnny Zeeman, and a woman was shot dead practically in front of us.

JUDY: **Right. That one's *Dying for a Clue*. My third novel.**

JENNIFER: Aren't you the prolific one.

JUDY: **Just answer the questions. Who knows? Some editor might read this and . . .**

JENNIFER: All right. But you make it sound like my involvement with so many murder cases is excessive. Actually, I agree, but I can't seem to do anything about it. You see, in a very real way, murder is my business. I write about it, and, in doing research for my books, I occasion- ally (Sam would say always) find myself where I shouldn't be.

JUDY: **Selling that first novel is difficult. How do you keep yourself positive, considering the number of rejec- tions you've received?**

JENNIFER: Dwelling on rejections never got anybody anywhere. I've written nine novels, and one of these days I'm actually going to sell one of them. I'm twenty-nine years old, and I've been writing ever since I got out of college. I heard an author speak one time who said, "Persistence is every bit as important as talent." I believe that. Besides, I've got too many years invested to give up now. All I need is that initial break. I figure, after that, I should be able to sell most of what I've written.

So, Judy, who did you say your editor was?

JUDY: **Later.**

JENNIFER: Promise?

JUDY: **It was part of the deal. Your critique group seems to be important to both your personal and professional lives. Do they really help with your writing?**

JENNIFER: Absolutely. I don't know what I'd do without them. They're all very talented, although they do have their problems.

JUDY: **How so?**

JENNIFER: Leigh Ann is a hopeless romantic. She can turn the most innocent encounters into . . . Let's just say, she has a vivid imagination. Teri writes romantic suspense. She's a sweetheart, really, but she can seem somewhat brusque to people who don't know her. And those who do. Actually, sometimes she's downright rude. But whenever I've asked her for a favor, she's always come through. Not always the way I might have envisioned it, but she gets the job done. April does children's books. It seems like she's always eating and always pregnant. And one of the gentlest souls I've ever known. And then there's Monique, who keeps a copy of her one published science fiction book on her coffee table. We're not close, but whenever I've really needed her, she's always been there for me. Like family. They're all like family.

JUDY: Both Leigh Ann and Teri write romance, Monique science fiction, and April children's stories. Can they really help you with your mysteries?

JENNIFER: They're good writers, all of them, if a little overly dramatic with the prose now and then. We all write popular fiction, which has the same demands regardless of genres: great openings, dynamic characters, and a quick pace. Most important, they're always honest, if not always tactful.

JUDY: A lot of the people who follow your adventures seem interested in your relationship with Sam. Can you give us an idea what the future may hold for the two of you?

JENNIFER: I don't like talking about Sam. I care a lot about him, but it's really none of your or anybody else's business.

JUDY: You haven't figured it out yet, have you?

JENNIFER: I really haven't. Sometimes we seem so close. But then . . . We just need some time to sort through our feelings and let our relationship develop naturally. Seems like we have more help and advice in that department than we need.

JUDY: What do you mean?

JENNIFER: Dee Dee is always trying to get me married off, and Teri and Leigh Ann tell me daily how I shouldn't let a guy like Sam get away. But it seems like every time we try to work out what we are to each other, another crisis comes up.

JUDY: Or another dead body?

JENNIFER: Exactly.

JUDY: Your dog Muffy seems to be a great part of your life. Can you tell us how you came to adopt her?

JENNIFER: Muffy is a retired racing greyhound. I got her through one of the greyhound adoption organizations. She's terrific. She reminds me there's more to life than writing and work, and she's an absolute sponge for attention. I adore her.

JUDY: In *Dying to Get Published,* you were arrested. What was it like in jail?

JENNIFER: I'd prefer not to talk about those few hours I spent incarcerated. Suffice it to say, I never want to go back.

JUDY: What do you see for yourself in the immediate future?

JENNIFER: Getting published, of course.

JUDY: Of course.

JENNIFER: Now, let's talk about how you made your first sale. And your agent's name. And your editor's.

❋

DYING FOR A CLUE

By Judy Fitzwater

To obtain some real-life investigative experience, Jennifer joins a private eye on an assignment. But when their late-night rendezvous explodes into murder, Jennifer finds herself high on the killer's hit list.

"DYING FOR A CLUE is a fast-paced, easy read that is entertaining and beguiling. No matter the genre, anyone who is an aspiring writer will identify with Jennifer and find her 'writing' situations remarkably familiar."

—*Romantic Times*

**Published by Fawcett Books.
Available in your local bookstore.**

❋